Other Books by Elmer Kelton

*forthcoming

CAPTAIN'S RANGERS

Elmer Kelton

A TOM DOHERTY ASSOCIATES BOOK
NEW YORK

This is a work of fiction. All the characters and events portrayed in this book are either products of the author's imagination or are used fictitiously.

CAPTAIN'S RANGERS

Copyright © 1968, 1996 by Elmer Kelton

A Forge Book
Published by Tom Doherty Associates, LLC
175 Fifth Avenue
New York, NY 10010

www.tor.com

Forge® is a registered trademark of Tom Doherty Associates, LLC.

ISBN: 0-812-57490-7

First Forge edition: August 1999

Printed in the United States of America

0 9 8 7 6 5 4 3

Author's Note

BETWEEN THE RIO GRANDE AND THE NU-
eces River lay a disputed region known in the 1800s as
the Nueces Strip, claimed by both Texans and Mexicans. It was a frequent battleground in an unofficial but
long-simmering conflict that continued spilling blood for
nearly forty years after the Mexican War officially ended
in 1846. It was to a considerable degree a racial war,
growing out of the same clash of vastly different cultures
that had led to the Texas revolution against Mexico.
Unreasoning racial hatred on both sides fostered a spirit
of lawlessness which tolerated and even encouraged free-
booters on both banks of the Rio Grande, men who
pillaged and killed in the name of either Texas or Mexico, victimizing the innocent of both races and calling
their acts patriotism.

Into this festering trouble spot in 1875 rode Captain
L. H. McNelly, a complex and dedicated man of frail
health but iron will, seeming to sense that he had only

a while to live, and determined to bring peace in that short time if he had to kill half the people in the Strip. A former officer in the Confederate army, McNelly had consented nevertheless to serve in the hated Texas State Police set up by the Union-dominated Reconstruction government in the hope that he could somehow serve justice despite the corrupted system. When the police were at last disbanded and the old Texas Rangers reorganized, the uncorrupted McNelly was awarded a captaincy.

In the Nueces Strip he and his Ranger company tracked down American and Mexican outlaws with equal dedication, disregarding race in a grim quest for law and order. His measures sometimes had an awful finality and may seem strong by today's standards, but they were acceptable to and expected by the people of his time, for nothing less would bring the brigands to heel. McNelly's bold raid across the border to strike an outlaw stronghold at Las Cuevas, below Rio Grande City, stirred the federal government into near panic and threatened for a time to breach relations between the United States and Mexico. But McNelly refused to back down from his tough stance and dealt a shattering blow to the border jumpers, bringing about a vital turning point in the long, undeclared war.

Though real peace was still years in coming, historians give McNelly and his Rangers major credit for the beginning of a better time.

One

THEY RODE HORSEBACK UP AUSTIN'S broad main thoroughfare toward the forbidding antebellum structure which now, ten years after the Civil War, was being denounced in the legislature as the worst firetrap and eyesore in Texas—the capitol building. There were two riders, a big man with a broad-brimmed Mexican border hat and a little man with a short brown beard. A vague military look—something sensed as much as seen, something about the way he carried himself—made it plain that the smaller man was the one in charge.

He rode up almost to the steps and swung down from the saddle. He paused a moment, his thin shoulders pinching as he coughed into one hand. His face was pale and sickly, but his piercing eyes saw all there was to see and gave a hint that behind them a keen mind was running with the whistle tied down. He handed the reins to the big man and said: "Stay close, Sergeant. I have no idea how long I'll be with the governor."

Two men idled on the steps, puffing cigars and arguing about an item in a newspaper. One looked up, frowning. "It's McNelly." He spoke in a voice the little man could not miss.

"McNelly?" The other snorted. "Ain't he the one used to work for them damned carpetbag State *Police?*"

McNelly gave no appearance of hearing until the big man took an angry stride toward the loafers. He turned and said, "No, Sergeant. There'll be no brawling on the capitol steps. They didn't say anything, and you didn't hear it."

The sergeant glared at the idlers but did not question the order. "Yes, sir, Captain." He watched Captain McNelly march into the building and out of sight.

The loafers felt that the order was their protection. One said, "The sergeant don't sound like a carpetbagger to me. Does he to you, Wilse?"

"Naw, he don't. Where you from, Sergeant?"

Anger stained the big man's face. He ignored the question until it was thrown at him a second time. "Arkansas," he replied curtly.

"Arkansas. Well, now, I wouldn't hardly think there'd be no carpetbaggers from Arkansas. I don't see any uniform, either. What kind of a sergeant are you, anyway?"

"Ranger sergeant. Texas Rangers."

"A Texas Ranger from Arkansas. That does beat all, don't it, Wilse? A carpetbag Texas Ranger sergeant from Arkansas."

The sergeant put one booted foot forward, caught himself and stepped back, glancing up at the open windows as if certain the captain would see him. Crisply he declared, "War's been over for ten years. There's no such of a thing anymore as a carpetbagger. Somethin' else, Captain never *was* one. The man who says different is a low-down, yellow-bellied liar. And he hasn't got the guts to come to the Ranger camp tonight and meet me out past the picket line."

"If a man *was* to come around, who would you send out to fight him? That consumptive-looking captain of yours?"

The sergeant moved forward, fists up. The loafer jumped to his feet. "Remember your orders, Sergeant."

The sergeant's eyes narrowed, and his voice went quiet, the way the air sometimes does just before a storm breaks loose. "I'll remember my orders. But I'll also remember you two. And if you're not on the picket line tonight to find me, I'll be around tomorrow to find you." He looked as if he could drive a nail with his bare hand. The loafers decided they were moths too close to the flame.

He watched, the color still high in his broad face, as the two retreated down the dirt street and disappeared into the open door of a saloon. He led the horses to a shady place and loosened the cinches, then squatted on the ground. There he could watch both the door of the capitol building and the door of the saloon. He would be here a long time, more than likely, but the captain had said wait.

When a man followed McNelly, he learned to rest every time he got the chance, for sometimes there was no rest at all. For a little man, Captain had the devil's own endurance, except when he was suffering one of his spells.

The sergeant half dozed in the gentle warmth of the spring morning, but every movement at the capitol door caught his eye. He was sure the loafers had not left the saloon, either.

After perhaps two hours, he saw the familiar gaunt figure pass through the doorway and start down the long steps, back straight, thin shoulders held proud. The sergeant led the horses forward. He could tell McNelly was troubled by the way he chewed his unlighted cigar. The sergeant boiled with curiosity, but a man never asked the captain unnecessary questions. If Captain wanted something known, he would tell it. If he chose to keep it to himself, all hell couldn't prize it out of him. His men learned to watch him and take their cue from his actions. If he ate a good supper, they knew they could figure on sleeping. If he drank coffee and munched a little hardtack, they knew a night ride was coming up, for Captain believed a man traveled best when he rode with his belly lank.

Captain asked, "Do you have any business in Austin that needs settling before we leave, Sergeant?"

The sergeant hadn't known they were going anywhere, but then, he doubted the governor had called McNelly in to talk about the old days of the Confederacy. "That depends, sir. I take it we'll be gone before tonight?"

"My orders are to leave when I'm ready. And I'm ready."

The sergeant frowned. "Well, sir, there *is* one little piece of business I ought to take care of. Won't be but a minute or two. I have a small debt that needs settlin' in that saloon."

"All right, but no drinking. We've got to ride."

"No drinkin', sir." The sergeant dismounted. He held the reins awkwardly until the captain silently reached out for them. Under no circumstances would the sergeant have presumed to *ask* Captain to hold his horse. He walked into the saloon.

Two minutes later he was back smiling, rubbing the knuckles of his right hand against his shirt. In his left hand he held several black cigars. "For you, Captain. Compliments of the bartender."

"Thank you, Sergeant. Debt all paid?"

"Paid in full, sir."

He knew better than to ask where they were going. But there were ways of fishing for an answer. "Spring like this, it could still get chilly up in North Texas. Somebody stole my coat. Reckon I ought to buy me a new one, sir?"

"We're not heading north." The little captain's sharp eyes held a rare glint of dark humor, and the sergeant knew McNelly saw through him. "We're going south."

"I didn't mean to pry, Captain."

"You had just as well know. I find the rumor is out anyway. The governor has authorized me to recruit new men and build up my force for a cleanup job. It'll be a dirty one."

The sergeant struggled against his curiosity, but he couldn't keep it from showing.

The captain could see. "We're going all the way to the Rio Grande. Our orders are to clean up the Nueces Strip."

Two

THEY CALLED IT THE NUECES RIVER,
but many of those early Texans didn't know how to spell
it, for they were *gringos* and the word was Spanish, given
for the pecans and other nut-bearing trees which grew
in wild abundance along its banks. To Anglo ears the
name sounded like New Aces, and that was how some
of them wrote it.

A map of Texas shows the Nueces is born amid the
Edwards Plateau, draining the limestone ridges and the
live-oak flats far west of San Antonio. It runs generally
south until it comes within less than forty miles of the
mud-choked Rio Grande. Then, like a skittish colt wary
of a tired old stallion's uncertain temper, it shies off and
quarters south-eastward, ever edging away from the big
river. It cuts across the horn-shaped lower tip of Texas
and spills itself into the Gulf's blue waters at the north-
ernmost point of Padre Island, a hundred miles above
the mouth of the Rio Grande.

That stretch of coastal prairie and desert wasteland, that parched region of short grass and cactus, mesquite and chaparral lying between the two rivers was known in Texas' youthful years as the Nueces Strip. By treaty it belonged to Texas, but the original people living there hadn't written the treaty. Most of them hadn't even read it. They lived in easy tempo in thatched huts and brush *jacales*, in rock houses and sun-baked adobes, raising their little patches of corn, running their rangy cattle on God's own grass. They ate *gringo* beef when it came handy, for taking from the *gringo* wasn't stealing; it was an act of liberation. They worshipped their God with a great devotion and loved their families as fiercely as they hated their enemies. Though they lived in Texas, they considered themselves Mexican. They had no particular allegiance to the government of Mexico, for it changed as often as the moon, but they honored Mother Mexico because they were of *la raza*, The Race.

Since the Mexican War they had found themselves crowded more and more by the light-skinned *extranjeros*, the foreigners who came with horses and cattle, with official-looking papers and with tough, badge-wearing *rinches* on horseback to enforce the foreign words on those papers. Some of the people of *la raza* retreated across the big river to simmer in anger and futility. Others stayed, for to them the land was as Mexican as themselves, and one did not leave his *querencia*—his homeland—any more than he would abandon his mother. The more tolerant made friends with individual Anglos, though they distrusted these blue-eyed ones as a race. *Mira, hombre*, is it not widely known that the *gringo* has but two aims in this world, to rob the man and to despoil the woman? The *gringo*, in turn, sometimes found that there was no more loyal friend than a Mexican who liked you, though he was convinced that as a group the "greasers" were un-

trustworthy. Why, man alive, anybody could tell you the
Mexicans were a cut-throat bunch of thieves and liars
you couldn't afford to turn your back on.

Small wonder, then, that for decades a minor, undeclared war flared spasmodically along the Nueces Strip,
sometimes fed on the one side by cow thieves and mur-
derers who justified themselves as patriots, fighting for *la
raza*; and fed on the other side by land grabbers and
Mexican-haters who eased whatever conscience they
may have had by telling themselves this was a holy war
that had started with the Alamo.

It reached its peak in the spring of 1875. That was
the year of McNelly's Rangers . . . of Palo Alto Prairie
and Las Cuevas. . . .

Vincente de Zavala missed his loop at the last calf's hind
legs, and chunky Bonifacio Holgúin, standing near the
mesquite-wood branding fire, began to hoot at him.
"*Cuidado, muchacho*, or you will rope your own neck and
strangle yourself. If it were your young wife in your
hands instead of that rope, you would not fumble so."

De Zavala told him in rich and fragrant Spanish to
go to hell. He had been dragging these calves out by
their heels. This time he built a new loop in his rawhide
reata and purposely roped the calf around the neck. It
bawled and pitched and kicked. Vincente's white teeth
gleamed in mischief. This, *hombre*, would give that sugar-
eating Bonifacio cause to laugh out of the other side of
his mouth.

Tall Lanham Neal cast a quick glance at the young
woman who stood watchfully by the branding irons,
right hand protected from the heat by a heavy leather
glove. Good thing all that hurrawing was covered up in
Spanish, he thought, for much of it was ripe and gamey.
But on reflection he knew Zoe Daingerfield probably

understood every word. She had spent her life among the people of the Nueces Strip.

He shrugged. *If she knows what it means, it's nothing new to her. If she don't, it won't do her no harm.*

Anyway, he had tried to tell her. He had tried to talk her out of coming with the men on cow hunts like this. It wasn't for a woman. But old man Griffin Daingerfield was hobbling around waiting for a broken leg to heal, and he had declared that one of the Daingerfields needed to be out looking after the family interests. The old man wouldn't have been on that crutch in the first place if he hadn't bullheadedly refused to let Vincente take the vinegar out of a fresh and rested young horse for him. Griffin, in short, was a great deal older than he was ready to admit.

There had been only one Daingerfield son, and he had been taken by the fever the year the Yankees tried to put their gunboats up the Rio Grande to stop Confederate cotton from crossing the Mexican border. Old Griffin had tried to bring up his daughter to take the boy's place and be able to inherit the ranch someday. He had done a fair-to-middlin' job of it, Lanham Neal thought. She was a cowgirl; you had to give her that. When she got her knee hooked over the horn of that sidesaddle—hidden by heavy riding skirts, of course—there wasn't any shaking her loose; she rode like a grass burr. She knew the cow. She could even rope a little, when she had to, though roping from a sidesaddle was not widely encouraged.

The hell of it was—and this must have bothered the old man—she still looked like a woman. A pretty good-looking woman, as far as a brush-country cowboy like Lanham Neal was concerned. Maybe she *wouldn't* have caused any stampede in a place like San Antone where pretty women grew like peaches on a tree, but down here she was like a single blossom on an empty prairie.

The old man had chased many a smitten cowhand away from his door, forbidding him ever to let his shadow fall there again. Lanham Neal had stolen many a long and wishful look at Zoe Daingerfield's quiet face, and now and again she looked back at him. But old Griffin never caught him at it; Lanham was careful about that.

Jobs weren't easy to come by these days; in this border country money was tight. Money was *always* tight for Lanham Neal. Seemed to him sometimes that hard luck dogged him the way a skulking wolf will trail after a lame bull, waiting to see him stumble. Seemed like every time Lanham had something going his way—something that looked as if it could work out well—luck would turn on him and kick him in the face. This job was good. Lanham didn't want to lose it, not even for a smile or two from Zoe Daingerfield.

Lanham stood aside and gave Bonifacio the honor of grabbing the fighting calf and flanking it, for it served him right. Bonifacio's heckling had needled Vincente into bringing this one by the neck instead of by the heels. Bonifacio swore profusely, threw his knee into the ribs as the calf jumped, then with great exertion brought it over and down hard on its side. The calf's breath gusted out with a harsh grunt. Lanham grabbed one hind leg and pulled it toward him, dropping on his rump and hooking the other hind leg firmly with the heel of his boot. With Bonifacio holding one end and Lanham the other, the calf was helpless.

Vincente grinned down from the saddle as he recoiled the reata. "Bonifacio, if you talked less you would have more strength to wrestle the cattle."

Bonifacio's answer was unrepeatable. Zoe Daingerfield, unconcerned, walked out with a hot running iron in the gloved hand. She ran the letter D onto the calf's hip, then added a diagonal line that made it the Daingerfield Slash D. She carried the iron back to the fire, peeled off the glove and returned with a sharp knife. She earmarked the calf with a deep underbit, then bent over and with two strokes of the blade turned the bull calf into a steer.

Lanham looked away uncomfortably as she did it. That was a job a woman shouldn't even *see*, he thought, much less actually *do*. Lots of people would have looked at her in horror. What were these young women coming to?

If it bothered Zoe, she didn't show it. Old Griffin had trained her to look at life with both eyes wide open and not cover facts with a veil. She wiped the blade clean on an old handkerchief. "Last one, Lanham?"

Lanham was the *caporál* here, the strawboss. But *vaqueros* like Vincente and Bonifacio didn't really need much supervision. They could have done about as well without him, and Lanham knew it. He only hoped old Griffin didn't come to the same conclusion. "Yes, ma'am, we're through. Your daddy is twelve calves richer."

"Twelve calves." She didn't sound particularly pleased. She watched as Bonifacio opened the gate and the cattle trotted warily out in single file, a couple of the cows feinting at Bonifacio with their sharp horns. "How many of those calves will we raise, and how many will be stolen across the river by the *Cortinistas?*"

Lanham shook his head. *"Quién sabe?"* His frowning gaze trailed the cattle. They clattered off toward the protection of a mesquite thicket, where the bewildered calves would pause to lick their wounds and the cows would make a motherly fuss over them. Lanham knew that for the drive the four riders had made today, they ought to have picked up a lot more cattle. Zoe had called it. The river, that was the trouble.

The Rio Grande lay just a few miles south. A *bandido* didn't have to be skilled at his trade to swim a horse across there in the dark of night, round up whatever stock came easy to hand and take them back over. They had done it in a minor way for years and years. Now they were doing it wholesale, riding across in bunches, stealing everything that walked on four legs except the jackrabbits and the wild *javalina* hogs. In their own eyes they were more than *bandidos* now; they were *Cortinistas*, "soldiers" of the general Juan Nepomuceno Cortina.

"Dad needs these cattle," Zoe said worriedly. "They're stealing him blind and he can't afford it."

"Damn little I see that he can do about it." Lanham gave her a boost up onto her sidesaddle. This was one thing which always gave him a valid excuse to touch her. "You all set, Miss Daingerfield?"

"All set. And you can call me Zoe." She smiled.

"Not when your old daddy's in earshot."

She smiled again. "He's miles away."

That was what made it frustrating, sometimes, to work here. Lanham Neal had had saloon girls and sidewalk *señoritas* smile at him lots of times, and it didn't fever him much. He answered their beckoning fingers now and then, when he felt the need, but he held no illusions about what they really wanted. They were after whatever silver might be jingling in his pockets; it never was very much. But with Zoe Daingerfield, it was different. She didn't need what little money could be found in a cowhand's pockets, but she smiled anyway. And that roused the fever in him.

It couldn't be for his money, because he didn't have enough to buy wadding for a shotgun. It wasn't likely his looks, either, for the cracked mirror in the *jacal* where he slept told him his mouth was too broad and his nose maybe a little too big. He almost always needed a haircut, and he didn't find time to shave very often. Perhaps Zoe saw something that didn't show in the mirror.

It might have been his strength she saw. Lanham Neal

had been over a lot of country the last ten or twelve years. At the age of fifteen, he had gone off hell-bent to fight the Yankees in the last futile months of the war, after they had killed his brother with Hood's army at Nashville. The first battle he was in, Lanham fell with a bullet through his hip before he ever got a good look at a Yankee. He had almost died. Long after the war was over, he started for home, penniless, walking most of the way in spite of the hip. And when he got got to where home had been, he found house caving in, family gone, the farm being worked by strangers who had taken it over for taxes in the name of the new Reconstruction government. In those first hard years after the war, a man could have swapped a good pair of boots for a farm . . . if he had had the boots. Lanham Neal was barefoot.

It had taken strength to make it through those times. One way and another, Lanham had survived. He had squatted on new land west of the old settlements, only to have the carpetbag lawyers take it away from him once he got it broken and a good crop of cotton almost ready to pick. He had gone to mavericking cattle— picking on those unbranded calves he figured came from herds the carpetbaggers had taken over. It was a practice considered legal enough in those times. No brand, no owner. When he had accumulated a good-sized bunch of calves and yearlings, he traded them for grown steers and threw the steers in with a Kansas-bound trail herd, figuring on filling his pockets with Yankee gold at the railhead. He never got there. Jay-hawkers stampeded the cattle at the Kansas line. Lanham wound up in a Kansas jail along with most of the other drovers when they tried to take their cattle back at gunpoint. They got away from those paper-collar Comanches with nothing but the clothes on their backs and a horse apiece to carry them home to Texas.

His luck had run with a startling consistency—always

sour. Everything he touched turned to ashes, seemed like.

That was one reason he hesitated to give much sign of his true feelings to Zoe Daingerfield. His luck might rub off on anybody who got too close to him.

There was another thing, too. Old Griffin Daingerfield liked him. Griffin had a head like a mule, sometimes. He was inclined to holler first and reflect later, but Lanham respected him too much to betray his trust. Griffin was one of the mossy-horned old brush-poppers who had taken this country like a challenge and had charged head-on, ready to fight man, beast, brush or weather, individually or in a bunch. Lanham figured a thing like that gave a man a right to holler once in a while. And beneath it all, the rancher had feelings for people—the ones he figured as *good* people; he made his own choices about that. Mexican or *gringo*, he sized them up individually and made his judgment. He seldom altered that first judgment. Lanham had come down to the Nueces Strip after the Kansas debacle, broke, all but barefoot again, the fever eating at him. If it hadn't been for Daingerfield and Zoe, the fever probably would have carried Lanham off for good. Griffin took the sick cowboy into his house and doctored and fed him. The only thing he had required—and he did that with looks and actions rather than with words—was that Lanham keep a fitting distance between himself and Zoe . . . no stirring of any emotions that might lead to something the old man would have to oil his rifle for. Lanham had kept that faith, though now and again it took strong measures like a sudden dip in the cold waters of a tank, or even an infrequent trip to the lamp-lighted streets of Brownsville and Matamoros.

Vincente de Zavala pointed toward the cattle as they disappeared into the brush. In Spanish he said, "It is good that we have them branded. When their mothers wean them, they might fall into the hands of maverick-ers."

Lanham's reply was in English. It was common for border people to conduct bi-lingual conversations, each person using the language that came easiest to him but understanding the other. "Griffin Daingerfield needs them as bad as any mavericker. Gettin' to be all he can do to hold this place together. He goes under, you and me are out of a job, Vincente. You with a young wife to feed, that wouldn't be good."

Vincente shrugged. "Food is not a woman's only need. Or a man's."

Bonifacio was staring back across the corral, his round, brown face puzzled. "*Caporál*, I thought the branding fire had burned itself out."

"It has, just about."

Bonifacio pointed. "It makes much smoke."

Lanham turned, frowning. It was smoke, surely enough, and at a glance he knew it didn't come from the branding fire. He rubbed a sleeve across his sweating face and cast a quick glance at Zoe. "Vincente, that is the direction of the house."

Zoe gasped, a cold fear suddenly rushing into her eyes.

"*Caporál* . . ." Vincente's mouth dropped open. "*Bandidos?*"

Lanham swore. "I hope not. Hang on, Zoe. We got to ride hard."

The words were wasted. She had already made the start.

Bonifacio was always the last to grasp an idea. He spurred mightily, but he never did catch up.

Vincente was saying over and over, "María!" It was the name of his wife. "That Cheno Cortina. That ac-cursed Cheno!"

*   *   *

He ruled the lower river country, at least that on the south bank of the Rio, this Cheno Cortina. Juan Nepomuceno Cortina was his full name, but to the people of *la raza* on both sides of the Bravo, he was Cheno, and for most of them the name carried a touch of magic. Of good blood but unschooled, shrewd and ambitious but without mercy for those who opposed him, the red-bearded one had repeatedly gouged the greedy *gringos*, hitting them in their moneybags where it really hurt and inviting them to kiss his backside. This in itself was enough to insure his endearment to all those shoeless ones who had lost land to the *extranjeros*, to all those *pobres* who had worked hard for little pay and had felt the contempt that sometimes lurked in narrowed *gringo* eyes.

In this spasmodic border war, *el generál* for more than a decade now had been Cheno Cortina, and his soldiers had been the *Cortinista* cattle rustlers and horse thieves, bush-whackers and house burners, darting across the river unpredictably, here one time, yonder another. Quiet for months, they would suddenly make a lightning guerrilla raid, leaving a trail of fire and blood, usually escaping across the river unscathed and carrying their booty of horses or cattle, or, once in a while, silver and gold. Now and again a few hapless ones failed to make it and lay till their bones bleached white in the Texas sun. But if ever they crossed to the south bank, they were in sanctuary, swallowed up by the immensity of Mexico, sheltered by sympathetic *peons* who considered them avengers of a great wrong—people who still cursed the day the vain tyrant Santa Anna had ingloriously lost at San Jacinto and to save his own bloody hide had signed away to the Texans a birthright the Mexicans considered their own.

Now other men rode and dared and sometimes died, while Cheno Cortina waited patiently in Matamoros and pulled the strings, basking in the sunshine of the people's admiration and growing rich from his share of the Texas spoils.

Vincente de Zavala hit the ranch yard ahead of the others. "María," he shouted, eyes searching desperately through the smoke. He was out of the saddle and on the ground running before his horse slid to a stop. In front of the charred *jacal* that had been his, a woman lay still and silent. The south wind picked up dust from the hoof-churned earth and tugged at the shredded remnants of her black dress. Vincente dropped to his knees. He cried out in anguish.

Zoe saw, and her face blanched. She ran for the smoking ruin of the "big house," which in reality hadn't really been very big. "Dad! Dad!"

No answer came. Lanham saw the reason before she did. He saw the crumpled figure lying in the yard.

Zoe screamed and jumped to the ground, turning her horse loose to stand or to run, whichever he chose. He would have run from the smoke had Bonifacio not spurred in and taken the reins. Lanham handed him his own and walked to the girl. She knelt by her father, trying to shake him to consciousness. Lanham could tell by looking that it was useless. Griffin Daingerfield was dead. There must have been a dozen bulletholes in his back.

There'll be some in the front, too, I expect, Lanham thought gravely. *He wouldn't have shown them his back until he fell.*

Bonifacio tied the horses and came trotting. Lanham turned and shook his head. Bonifacio crossed himself and went to try to comfort Vincente.

Lanham looked toward the big house and saw the old man's crutch lying there in front of it. He could see the wink of brass cartridge cases, scattered about. Griffin had made it to here without his crutch, probably firing his rifle all the way. The rifle was not in sight. The raiders undoubtedly had taken it.

Lanham's eyes went to fire as he looked helplessly down at the sobbing girl. *Damn it all, what can a man say? What can he do? That luck of mine, rubbing off again.*

Pale, Bonifacio stood with sombrero in his hand beside the quietly grieving Vincente. He looked as awkward and lost as Lanham felt, for he wasn't doing Vincente any good and didn't know how to start.

Bonifacio suddenly stiffened and looked at Lanham. He came trotting, the sombrero still in his hands. Lanham reached to his hip for the reassuring feel of his pistol, for the thought hit him that Bonifacio had seen something.

But Bonifacio had *thought* of something. "*Caporál*, I just remembered. We have not seen Hilario."

Hilario Gomez was an old retainer who had already been a graying *vaquero* when Griffin Daingerfield had first come into this country. Gomez had worked for him, helped him establish himself here. Too old now to ride or to do heavy work, Hilario mostly hung around the place, doing minor fix-up jobs and giving freely of his advice, telling the hands such as Vincente and Bonifacio that nowhere today did one find *vaqueros* like those of old, like those he had ridden with in the days of his youth.

Bonifacio trotted around the yard, shouting, "Hilario! Hilario!"

Lanham's first thought was that the *viejo* might have run away at sight of the *Cortinistas*. But he rejected that idea, for despite the differences in their upbringing and their viewpoints, Hilario and Griffin had been much alike. Neither ever turned his back on trouble. If anything, they had seemed to thrive on a certain amount of it, so long as it did not come in excess. Lanham joined Bonifacio in the search.

They found the *vaquero* lying against a corral fence near a smouldering barn. His old cotton shirt was stained with blood, and his eyes were glazed, but breath still came erratically. *"Quién es?"* he gasped. *Who is it?*

"He hears us," Lanham told Bonifacio, "but he can't see us." He spoke in Spanish to the old man, who had stoutly refused to learn English. "Be not afraid, uncle. It is Lanham and Bonifacio. We have come to help you."

"María . . . el patrón . . ." The words came through grinding pain.

No use lying to him, Lanham thought. "Only you are still alive." *And not by very much, either.*

He turned Hilario over gently and saw the two bullet wounds in the thin chest. Anyone else would have died, he thought. But they had raised them tough in Hilario's day, like the mesquite and the cactus. "Bonifacio, let's carry him down into the yard, to the shade. I doubt there's anything left to treat him with, but we'll look."

Carefully they lifted the old man, trying not to hurt him any more than they could help. They set him down beneath the broad, sheltering cover of a brush arbor that the *bandidos* somehow hadn't bothered to burn. Lanham tore the shirt away and grimaced. The bullets were still in there. He had nothing to extract them with except a pocketknife, and that would surely kill the old man. Small chance he had of living anyway.

In a hoarse voice Hilario started trying to tell what had happened. "Hush, Hilario," Lanham said. "Don't waste yourself talking. Save your strength."

The old man paid him no mind. It occurred to Lanham that he never had; Hilario regarded the younger generation—Mexican or Anglo—with no more than a quiet tolerance. He kept on talking, telling how it had been. The raiders had caught him unawares. In the old days they would not have done it, he said, but nowadays his ears had been failing him, and he was occupied with

cleaning the picket-built barn. They had been upon him
before he had known they were in the country. He had
had no weapon, other than the pitchfork in his hands.
He had run at them with that, but he had not taken
three steps before they brought him down.

Through the dust and the pain, he had seen María
dragged out of her *jacal*. She had pulled free. Yipping
and shouting like coyotes after a pullet, some of the men
had grabbed her. Old Griffin had boiled out of the big
house, dragging himself without the crutch, firing as rapidly as he could lever his rifle. He had died in a matter
of moments. María had not died quickly, or easily. The
old man had pulled himself to the corral fence, but that
had been as far as he could move. He could only lie and
listen.

Old Hilario's sightless eyes wept bitter tears, and his
gnarled hands clenched weakly as he went on about how
different it would have been when he was a young man
in all his strength, a man to make *bandidos* tremble for a
hundred miles up and down the Rio. Lanham tried to
quiet him, but Hilario talked until the last of his strength
was gone. And with the last of his strength, the life ebbed
out of him, too.

Bonifacio quietly crossed himself. "God was not looking this way today." Shock lay in his eyes. "I can see
why they would kill Hilario, for he came at them with
the pitchfork. They hated the *patrón* for his blood. But
why should they kill María? She could not hurt them,
and she was of the same blood as they."

"She lived on a *gringo* ranch. That made her one of
us, not one of them." Lanham carefully placed Hilario's
limp hands on his chest and smoothed what he could of
the rumpled shirt. "Been thirty years since the war with
Mexico. You'd think it was still on."

Bonifacio said, "For some, it has never finished."

Lanham's eyes still burned. The smoke, he figured.

He walked back to Vincente. The *vaquero*'s face was buried in his woman's long black hair. Lanham touched the man's shoulder. "Vincente, this won't do you any good. We'll go and fetch some help."

Slowly Vincente's head came up. His black eyes were wet, but behind the tears lay glowing coals. "There is no help for her. Is there any help for the *patrón*, or for Hilario?"

Lanham shook his head. "They have all gone together. There is no one to help now but *la patrona* . . . Zoe."

Stricken, Vincente gazed at the lifeless olive face. When they killed María, they had murdered two, for she was carrying Vincente's child. Vincente's eyes were closed, and his voice was down almost to a whisper, but it carried thorns. "There will be no help for the ones who did this, *caporál*."

Zoe Daingerfield left her father and staggered across to stand by the men. Tears streamed down her face, but vengeful anger was beginning to show. "What do you mean, Vincente?"

"We will go after them," Vincente rasped. "We will kill them!"

Lanham's fists were tight. "I wish we could." But he saw little hope of it. Retribution had overtaken few of Cheno's men. "There was a sizable bunch of them. By the tracks, maybe twenty. Even if we was to catch up to them, what could we do?"

"Slit every throat we could get our hands on."

Bonifacio protested. "Against so many? We would not last three minutes."

Vincente eased his wife's body gently to the warm earth. He raised his eyes, his voice quivering with rage. "It will be a glorious three minutes. We will kill as many as we can."

Zoe Daingerfield surprised Lanham most. "He's right, Lanham. We're wastin' time."

"We?"

"They had a long start before we got here. We'll have to ride like hell to catch them."

"Zoe, you're not goin' anyplace. Leastways, not after them bandits. They'd do to you what they done to María."

"They killed my father."

"And they'd kill *you* without blinkin' twice."

Vincente began calculating. "They took the *patrón*'s horses. Likely they will want to take some of his cattle, too. If that be so, they cannot move fast. The *patrona* does not go; she stays here. But *I* go. Do you go with me, *caporál*? And you, Bonifacio?"

The bitterness of it all was flooding over Lanham now. "I'll go."

Bonifacio stared at the ground, trembling like a man beneath a noose. "My mother lives in Matamoros, and my brothers. If I went with you, *el Cheno* would slaughter my people like cattle."

Vincente accepted the decision without rancor, though it was plain that Bonifacio's worry was not altogether about his family. "Then you will take *la patrona* to safety. You will go to town and bring help."

Bonifacio nodded. "Your María and the *patrón*, they must not be left lying here. They must be buried. Shall we wait until you come back?"

Vincente took a final look at the tiny figure that had been María. "Do not wait for me. Perhaps I will never come back."

Zoe caught Lanham's hand. "I am not going with Bonifacio. My place is here, with Dad and María and Hilario. I will stay." Lanham started to protest, but he saw something in her eyes, something like he had seen in Vincente's. Zoe said, "Go, Lanham. Kill them! Kill as many as you can!"

Vincente swung into his big-horned Mexico saddle and spurred out without looking back. He headed straight south, with the tracks. Lanham Neal mounted as quickly as he could, but Vincente was already a hundred yards ahead of him. It took a long time for Lanham to catch up.

Three

STRAIGHT AS THE CROW FLIES, IT WOULD have been something like ten miles to the Rio Grande. The horses had been ridden all day, and they didn't have it in them anymore to cover the ground very fast. Lanham feared he and the seething Vincente might kill both mounts if they kept pushing them at this pace all the way to the river.

Almost simultaneously, both men saw the tracks that led away from the main trail of horses and cattle. Vincente's eyes narrowed in suspicion. Lanham swung to the ground and found a dark blotch in the midst of a flat impression in the sand. Blood.

Vincente said, "They laid a man down."

Lanham made a grim smile. "Old Griffin was always a good shot. They didn't get him at no bargain." Looking up, he pointed to where tracks of three horses led away through the chaparral. "They probably figured this one was wounded too bad to make it to the river. There's a little *rancho* over yonderway."

Vincente spat. "Galindo's *rancho*. That Galindo, *no vale nada*. It does not surprise me that they go to him." Vincente's voice rasped. "If he has helped them, I will nail his hide to Cheno Cortina's own door."

Lanham knew the place. Galindo had a patch of corn, a few cattle and a herd of children. Old Griffin had mentioned more than once that the *muchachos* looked well fed; and he strongly suspected it was being done on Daingerfield beef. He had also suspected Galindo was branding his mavericks, as many as he could lay a reata upon. Some places in Southern Texas, that suspicion would have been enough to leave a Mexican *ranchero* dangling from the limb of a stout tree, for cattlemen as a class were not noted for long patience with thieves. But Daingerfield didn't work that way. Had he ever caught Galindo skinning a Daingerfield animal or putting his own brand on a Slash D brute, he would have shot him dead on the spot and never looked back. He would not do it on suspicion. "Patience," he had counseled. "Give them enough rope and they'll tie the noose in it theirselves."

The tracks led straight to the brush *jacal*. Rifle in his hand, Vincente rode almost to the door, carefully watching the dwelling. He motioned toward the tracks. "Three horses came, two left. I see a horse in that brush corral. That would belong to the *bandido*."

Lanham drew his pistol and swung to the ground, crouching. Cautious, he looped the reins around the branch of a thin mesquite. Vincente simply dropped his reins and let his horse go. It wouldn't travel far without him; he had it trained to stand where the reins fell.

The shack was of brush and mud, except for the door of rough-sawed lumber. Rifle pointed straight ahead,

Vincente strode to the door and unceremoniously kicked it in. He plunged into the *jacal*. Lanham followed right behind him, heart pounding. He half expected to be shot point-blank.

Nothing happened. A frightened Mexican family huddled against a mud wall . . . a mother, a daughter almost grown, several other children ranging down to four or five years. No man.

Vincente shouted in Spanish, "He is here somewhere! Where do you hide him?"

A bed of mesquite limbs and stretched cowhide was the only furniture other than a couple of benches and a table. The bed was big enough for a *bandido* to hide under. Vincente took two strides forward and kicked the corner posts away. The bed fell. A baby squawled and crawled out from under it. Vincente was keyed to such a furious pitch that he almost shot the baby before he could stop himself. He stood numb, staring.

Lanham pulled a blanket off of the bed. Beneath it, the cowhide showed a telltale sign. Lanham glanced at Vincente and saw agreement in the *vaquero*'s eyes. Blood.

Vincente whirled on the women. "Where is he?"

The women stared in terror. The children wailed.

"Where?" Vincente demanded again. He slashed out with his rifle and sent the table spinning against a wall. One leg broke off. He kicked the benches over onto the dirt floor. "Where?"

Galindo's wife collapsed to her knees in hysteria. The oldest daughter wrapped her arms around her mother and screamed at Vincente and Lanham.

Lanham said, "Galindo must've taken him out to try and hide him in the brush. We'll find him."

"Yes," Vincente said, and his voice was terrible. "We'll find him."

The sight of the terrified women and children unnerved Lanham a little, though it seemed to have no effect upon Vincente. The Mexican turned on his heel and strode outside. "There will be footprints."

There were, but too many of them. There were barefoot tracks the children had left in play, and tracks the women had made between the shack and the outdoor oven, and around the well. There were the tracks Galindo had made back and forth from the brush-covered arbor that served as a barn of sorts. Lanham looked under the arbor but saw no man.

Vincente shouted, "*Caporál,* over here."

Lanham went in a long trot. Silently Vincente showed him fresh *huarache* tracks, leading down toward a small corn patch. Following them, they saw a man coming up from the direction of the field, a hoe over his shoulder. Lanham knew Galindo by sight but no better than that. The *ranchero* attempted to give a pleasant Mexican welcome, but the anxiety was too strong not to betray him. "My house is your house." His lips smiled. His face broke out in cold sweat. "Why has God sent you here today?"

"Not God," Vincente replied tightly. "The devil. Where did you hide him, Galindo?"

"Hide who? The devil?"

Vincente rammed the rifle into Galindo's belly. "Do not play games with me, Galindo, or I will blow your guts out."

Galindo panicked and tried to dodge away. In doing it, he brought the hoe around. Vincente did not hesitate. The rifle roared. The hoe went sailing, and Galindo hit the ground on his back. Vincente dropped the muzzle as if to fire again. Lanham stopped him. "I don't think he meant to hit you, Vincente. Don't make a mistake you may be sorry for."

Vincente's face was as near white as it could ever be. "When one kills the likes of Galindo, it is never a mistake." But he raised the muzzle and stepped over the downed *ranchero*, not looking back. He walked briskly toward the field.

Lanham glanced once over his shoulder toward the *jacal*. The oldest daughter was running down toward them crying, "Papa! Papa!" Lanham could see she carried no weapon and was no threat. Galindo was rapidly passing the point of being able to raise up, much less to hurt anybody. Lanham turned and trotted after Vincente.

They came almost to the edge of the field. Vincente raised his hand as a signal to stop. He pointed wordlessly to a huge cluster of prickly pear, then toward a set of fresh footprints. The same *huarache* tracks, left by Galindo. Lanham nodded and made a sign which told Vincente to hold up while he circled around to the other side of the pear thicket. Vincente waited. Lanham moved with care, in a crouch. He could not see into the thick growth of pear, but he realized as his tongue moved across dry lips that the *bandido* might damned sure be able to see out. He remembered that time in the war when he had been shot in the hip, and the thought brought him no comfort.

A pistol fired and Lanham jumped backward by reflex. Cold dread wrapped itself around him. The bullet had missed, but he knew it had been aimed at him. He could see the curl of black smoke, but he still couldn't see the bandit.

Lanham fired once, as much by instinct as by design, and then moved fast. *If he gets me, he'll have to hit a moving target . . . moving like hell.* The bandit fired again. A puff of dust kicked up in front of Lanham.

Vincente waded heedlessly into the pear, his high-topped boots taking the thorns. His rifle roared, and Lanham heard a man cry out. Lanham moved quickly. He saw the bandit now, lying on his back in a small opening with the thick stand of prickly pear, trying vainly to raise his pistol. Black rage boiled in Vincente's face, and he cursed furiously. His rifle roared again. The bandit fell back threshing, all consciousness gone like the blowing-out of a candle, but the body still clutched at life. Vincente levered another cartridge into the breech and fired again. He fired and fired and fired, till there was not enough left of the bandit for a mother to recognize. When his last cartridge was spent and the hammer fell harmlessly, Vincente staggered back a step, crying like a child.

Lanham left him alone. He stood and waited till the outburst had run its course and Vincente stood in silence, the tears still running unashamedly down his cheeks. Only then did Lanham step forward. "You done all you could here. We better get ridin', *amigo*."

They walked back up the trail toward the *jacal*. The girl cradled her father's head in her arms and stared at them in wide-eyed terror. "No, no!" She cried in Spanish, "Please do not shoot him again."

Best Lanham could tell, looking down on the *ranchero*, was that the bullet had gone through the shoulder. With luck, and barring infection or bleeding to death, he ought to pull through and give his wife a few more children before he crossed over finally to the other side of that much bigger river.

Vincente's hands tightened on the rifle, and Lanham thought the *vaquero* might finish Galindo where he lay. "You'll run out of shells," Lanham suggested gently.

Vincente considered a moment, spat and moved on. Lanham glanced back and saw the girl's big brown eyes set on him in fear. He had never seen that kind of fear in a woman's face before. It reached him somewhere inside and made him feel cold. He figured she hadn't understood what he had said to Vincente in English; she thought Lanham was likely to shoot Galindo after all. He spoke to her in her own language. "If he went across

the Rio Grande, he would have a better chance of living
to be an old man."

She trembled. "But our home . . ."

"If you stay, he may be buried here, and much sooner
than he would like."

Lanham untied his horse and rode out to catch Vincente's, which had shield off a short way at the sound
of the shots. When he went back, he found Vincente
herding Galindo's wife and children outside. Vincente
reached into the outdoor fireplace and took out a burning stick. He shoved it against the *jacal* until the dry
brush began to blaze. In a moment the shack crackled
with flames. The dancing fire was reflected in Vincente's
bitter eyes when he turned to the chunky woman who
was Galindo's wife. "If ever another bandit asks you for
help, remember this day and tell him to ride on. And
one thing more: if ever I should come this way again
and find Galindo here, I will kill him."

He turned to Lanham and reached for his reins. "*Caporál*, I am ready to go."

Dusk came upon them before they reached the river.
Following the cattle tracks, they found a limping steer
the border jumpers had left straggling. Across its side
sprawled a huge Slash D, branded generously, the way
only a Mexican *vaquero* would do it. "One of mine,"
Vincente remarked. It was all he said.

The tracks led finally down the bank and into the
river. Across, Lanham could see a pinpoint of firelight.

"I reckon," he said, "they got away."

Vincente shook his head. "It is but a shallow river. I
have crossed it a hundred times."

Lanham knew Vincente intended to do it again. A
line on a map didn't mean much to a Mexican. For that
matter, it didn't mean much to Lanham, either. "You
want to go, Vincente? I'll go with you."

Vincente gravely shook his head. "The fight goes on, but from here it is to be my fight, not yours."

"Griffin was my boss, and my friend."

"But you are a *gringo*. Your face would get you killed, as soon as someone saw you in the daylight and knew you were not of the *renegados*."

"There's *gringo* renegades over yonder. I've seen them."

"But they are known, and they are safe. Your face would mark you. Me, I am one of the people. No one will look twice at me."

"You're just one man. Damn little you can do by yourself."

"Each of them is just one man, too, when they separate. I will go, and I will find them out. And then, one at a time . . ." He drew his knife and ran his finger along the edge of it.

"How long do you think you'll last, Vincente?"

Vincente shrugged. "Long enough, perhaps." He stared at the flickering firelight on the other side. "I want to live long enough to spill the blood of those who killed María. After that . . ." He held his silence a while. "I think the *patrona*, she will need you now, *caporál*. She is strong, but she is still a woman. A woman should not be alone."

"She'll have a hard time for a while."

"It is a hard world for everybody." Vincente shoved out his hand, and Lanham solemnly took it. Vincente said, "Perhaps I will see you again on this side of the river. If not, then I will see you in hell."

"Don't be in no hurry," Lanham replied. He swung down and stood watching Vincente disappear into the night, riding downriver a way to escape surveillance when he crossed over.

Four

CAPTAIN MCNELLY WAS A RESTLESS MAN.
He had a chair and a recruiting table set up in front of
the tent, but he strode back and forth beneath the deep
shade of a huge old live-oak tree. In front of him, several
men awaited their turn to be interviewed. Behind him,
men already accepted were making camp around the
wagon. Most of them were young men, some not even
able yet to grow a beard. They were a varied crew, but
the majority shared two trademarks. Their clothing was
common, generally well worn, for these were not flush
times in Texas. And without exception, each man had
a six-shooter on his hip. Most of them in addition carried
a rifle or a shotgun.

The slight captain chewed absently on a cigar he had
never bothered to light. His intense dark eyes studied a
young man who stood nervously before him. "Name?"

"Joe Benson."

"Occupation?"

"Cowboy, mostly. Farmed a little."

"Do you own that horse you've been riding? Is that your own pistol you carry?"

"Yes, sir."

"How good are you with the pistol?"

"Fair to middlin', sir. I've won some bets." He caught himself. "Not that I'm a bettin' man by nature, sir. I'm not atall."

"You don't appear old enough to have seen service in the late war. Have you had any military experience, or even been a peace officer?"

"No, sir, never did. My pa went to war, and a couple of my brothers, but I was still a barefooted young'un." He paused. "I *would* have gone to war, sir, if they'd let me. I run away once to join, but they tanned my britches. I wasn't but twelve."

It was usually difficult to read judgment in Captain's eyes. He carried a perpetual severity like some men carry a cane. "Have you ever had to use a gun against a man?"

"I fought Indians, sir, once on a trail job up through the Territory."

"Kill any?"

"No, sir. But they didn't kill me, either."

"Why do you want this job, Benson?"

"I'm broke, Captain."

"If you weren't broke, would you consider being a Ranger?"

The cowboy was slow to answer. "I couldn't rightly say, Captain. I'd think on it some."

The captain glanced at the sergeant, who sat at the table, watching. "That's an honest answer. Sign him on, Sergeant."

The next man was older. He had sat cross-legged on the ground, relaxed and awaiting his turn. He pushed slowly to his feet and walked forward with confidence.

The captain's sharp eyes quickly took in the polished pistol at his hip, the broad shoulders, the hard grin in the big man's face. "I'll save you some time, Captain," the applicant spoke up without waiting to be asked. "My name's Gabe Gribbon. This is my own pistol, and that good dun yonder is my horse. I got my own rifle. I can hit a man between the eyes as far as from here to that wagon yonder, and I've done it once or twice."

The captain turned the cigar slowly in his mouth, his eyes narrowed. He had to raise his chin to see the man's face, but somehow Captain gave the impression that he never really looked up to anybody. "I take it you've had military experience, then?"

"No, sir. Happened I was in Mexico durin' the late conflict. Business down there; seemed like I couldn't hardly get loose. But after the war I come back. I was with the State Police. I had lots of experience lawin', Captain. I've handled the rough ones."

A frown started to furrow the captain's thin face. "State Police, you say?"

"Yes, sir, Captain. Just like you."

The frown deepened. "You weren't in any outfit I ever served with."

"I served under Captain Helm. He was one that knowed how to make them stand up and pay attention. I learned a lot from him. *I* can make them Meskins look sharp and speak soft, I guarantee."

The captain slowly took the cigar from his mouth and worked up spittle. He turned his head to let it go. Then his eyes met Gribbon's. "I don't have a place for you."

The man sputtered. "No place for *me*? You been here all day signin' up cowboys and plowboys that ain't ever shot a man or been shot at in their lives, and you say you got no place for a man with my experience?"

"That is correct, Mister Gribbon. Not for a man with *your* experience."

Gribbon's face darkened. "I know what it is. It's the State Police. You're down on me because I was in the State Police. But you can't tar me with that brush, McNelly, without splashin' tar on yourself. I was just a private in that outfit, but you was a captain. You was a State Policeman, just like me."

"Not like you, Gribbon. God forbid that I was ever like you. Now, I've told you I can't use you. I have other men to interview."

"You can't just . . ."

The captain's face suddenly seemed to take on full color, and his eyes went hard. "Get out, Gribbon." His voice didn't rise, but it cut like a knife. "Git!"

Gribbon outweighed the captain by a hundred pounds. He carried a pistol, and the captain's was in the tent. But Gribbon seemed to shrink under that hard, cold stare. He began backing away, grumbling. "Damndest thing I ever seen. Let the word out that they're needin' Rangers, but when a *man* shows up they don't want him. Hell of an outfit this is goin' to be anyway, a bunch of left-handed, wet-nosed kids, led by a sawed-off runt that probably ain't got the strength to h'ist a keg of whisky onto his shoulder." He turned to his horse and started tightening the cinch he had loosened while he had waited his turn. He was still talking to himself.

"Gribbon!" a firm voice said behind him. He turned. Captain stood there, a pistol in his belt. His hands were not on the butt of it, but he made a point of showing he had it. The captain pointed to a hill which lay in the west.

"How long, Gribbon, do you think it would take a man to get to that hill and ride over it?"

Gribbon shrugged. "Ten minutes."

"I'll give you five!"

Five

IT HAD BEEN A LONG, CRUEL DAY, AND
Lanham Neal was wrung out. So was his horse. He
moved back from the river as the daylight rapidly faded.
It was a long way to the ranch, to Zoe Daingerfield. He
dreaded the ride. Hunger gnawed at him, but he knew
there would be nothing to eat at the burned-out ranchhouse. He thought of the crippled steer he and Vincente
had seen. At least there was beef, if he could find it
before dark folded in around him.

Back-tracking, he located the animal. He noted with
satisfaction that the injury was new, and to a forefoot.
That wouldn't taint the hindquarters any. He was
tempted to shoot the steer, but on reflection he thought
he was still too close to the river to be drawing unnecessary attention to himself. He let down his rawhide
rope. The steer tried to run into the brush, but it
couldn't move fast. Lanham took a quick swing, dropped
the loop around the horns, flipped the rope across the

steer's rump and rode away fast. The steer went down with a hard thump. Before it could arise, Lanham was there afoot, the knife in his hand.

In a little while he was riding north, a hindquarter hanging from each side of the saddlehorn, the hide still on it to keep it clean.

For no good reason he could think of, except that some inner compulsion drew him, he angled toward the Galindo place. A dozen times he had thought about the way Vincente had gunned the *ranchero* down. Lanham couldn't blame the *vaquero;* in his place and state of mind he might have done the same. Still, Lanham had been brought up with the belief that a suspect was innocent until proven guilty. The border country put a heavy strain on that kind of credo, but Lanham still had a little of it left, tattered though it was. Vincente's training, perhaps, had been along a vein much used and abused in Mexico ever since the time of the Spanish conquest: spare not the innocent, lest the guilty go unpunished.

He could see a dim glow in the place where the Galindo shack had been. Beyond it, fire burned in the outdoor fireplace. The women didn't see Lanham, or even hear him, until the dim light of the fire picked him up. The children screamed and ran for darkness. The women huddled fearfully beside a spread-out blanket where Galindo lay. Lanham didn't reach for his gun. He doubted seriously that anybody here had one; he doubted even more that they would have used it if they had it. He sat on the horse and looked down at Galindo. He did not see him move.

"Is he dead?" he asked in Spanish.

Señora Galindo began to pray, crossing herself. The girl pushed to her feet, trembling. "He lives. Did you come to kill him?"

"Don't you think I ought to? He was helping a bandit who had a part in the killing of three people at the Daingerfield ranch today. By all rights Vincente should have finished killing him awhile ago. And I should do it now."

The girl's voice was thin. "My father had no part in it. They came, bringing the wounded man. They told my father to hide and protect him, for he could not live to the river. They said if he did not do this, they would come back and kill my father and take us to slave for them across the Rio."

Lanham stared hard at the girl, wanting to believe it. It wasn't a new story, exactly. For years the bandits from the other side had harassed much of the Mexican population here almost as much as they harassed the *gringos*. To them you could be only one of two ways: for them or against them. If you were not for them, and you happened to be Mexican, that compounded your sin, for it meant that besides whatever else you had done or not done, you had betrayed your own.

Bad enough to be a *gringo*. Worse yet to be a traitor.

"You must believe me," the girl insisted. "I tell you the truth."

Lanham looked hard at the still form of Galindo. He was almost certain the *ranchero* had been mavericking Daingerfield cattle. Whether he was one of the organized bandits or not, he was a thief. The country would be well rid of him.

The girl pleaded, "Please, do not kill him. We will give you anything we have."

Lanham's gaze swung back to her. Her eyes were begging him. He jerked his thumb at the burned-out *jacal*. "I don't see that you have anything to give."

The girl was silent a moment, staring gravely at her father. Finally she raised her eyes. In the firelight, Lanham could see the tears. "If you will spare him, *I* have something to give."

Lanham guessed later that he was too tired and too

hungry, for what she said didn't soak in. "What do you mean?"

Trembling, she began to show anger. "You know. Must you make me shame myself before my mother and my father?"

Lanham leaned back in the saddle, taken by surprise. For a moment no words came to him. "I won't kill him," he said finally. "You can keep your virtue." He peered out into the darkness, where he could hear the children whimpering. "Those *muchachos* had anything to eat?"

The girl shook her head. Everything in the shack had been destroyed. Lanham slipped one of the hindquarters from the saddlehorn. "Their father has fed them plenty of Daingerfield beef before. The flavor won't come as any surprise to them."

He rode off into the night, somehow feeling as if he had been taken to a losing in a bottom-of-the-deck poker game. Least he could have done would have been to stay there and make them fix him some beef off of that hindquarter. But suddenly he had wanted to leave more than he wanted to eat.

The girl's tears stayed with him. They bothered him a lot worse than the sight of Galindo lying there wounded. Galindo had more than earned anything that had happened to him. The more Lanham thought about it, the less he figured Galindo deserved a daughter who would offer herself to save him.

The moon came up, finally, and it was welcome, though Lanham could have found the ranch in the dark. All he had to do was strike a trail he knew and stay with it. The horse would have gotten him there anyway, for horses have a keen instinct about going home.

It was eerily quiet and dark. Lanham rode up close and stopped awhile to listen. Times like these, it didn't pay to ride blindly into a place. He heard nothing. He thought of Zoe, and he knew what he had realized from the beginning, that he shouldn't have left her here by herself. But there had been no one to leave with her, and she would not go to town. It had been unthinkable to take her along when he and Vincente rode after the bandits. It would have been equally unthinkable for them to have stayed and not attempted any pursuit. He doubted that anyone could have slipped up on Zoe. She would have been hard to surprise, and once in the brush even harder to find.

He heard nothing to make him suspicious, so he touched spurs gently to the horse's ribs and started out of the brush toward the dim glow that had been the main house.

A chilling metallic click made him haul up on the reins and drop low in the saddle. "Zoe?" he spoke quickly.

"Lanham? Is that you?"

His heartbeat had quickened, and he found his breath unexpectedly short. "It's me, Zoe. Don't you pull that trigger."

"You ought to've sung out."

"I thought of it. But I also got to thinkin' what might happen if I found the wrong people here."

"I came within an inch of shooting you. I wouldn't have missed." She stepped out of the brush and into the moonlight, where he could see her. She stood in her riding outfit—the only clothes she owned now, since the fire—the rifle slack in her hands. She looked behind Lanham, into the brush. "Where's Vincente?"

"He didn't come back."

"They didn't . . ."

"No, they didn't kill him."

"Did you catch up to them?"

"They got across the river ahead of us, Zoe. All but one."

"And him?"

"He's crossed his last river."

She nodded grimly. "I'm glad. I just wish it could've been a dozen of them." She looked at the beef hanging from his saddlehorn. "What's that you got there?"

"A quarter off of one of your steers. You hungry?"

She blinked, seeming surprised. "I hadn't thought about it, but I guess I am."

"I'm as lank as a whippoorwill. We'll stir us up a fire and start a little *barbacoa*." He looked across the vacant yard. It seemed strange, no building left intact, not even a brush *jacal*. He could see the skeleton of the big house, the charred remains of two walls standing like dark ribs against the rising moon. "Nobody showed up yet?"

She shook her head. "Long ways to town. I expect it'll be daylight or better before Bonifacio gets back with help, even if they ride all night."

He gathered dry brush and started a fresh fire, well away from the burned house, well away from the arbor where the bodies lay. He turned his back, trying not to think of them. He cut green mesquite limbs for spits to cook strips of steak. He seated himself on the ground, gazing silently into the fire. Zoe sat beside him. She had never been this close to him before, and he wished the circumstances could have been different. He had wanted her like this for a long time. But there had always been old Griffin.

"You feelin' all right, Zoe?" he asked at length. "I mean, it's closer to the Bailey ranch, over west, than it is to town on the east. I could take you to Bailey's."

"No, Lanham. This is my place now. I won't leave it."

"I don't mean for good. Just for a few days . . . just to get away from here till things settle down."

"Things won't settle down, not till somebody's paid in blood for what happened today. I've made up my mind to that."

"You're a woman, Zoe. Ain't much a woman can do about it."

"I can ride. I can shoot. I can protect what belongs to me. And believe me. Lanham, I'll sure as hell do it."

Angry talk, he figured. Sure, Griffin had brought her up tougher than the average girl. He had tried to make a cowboy of her. But basically she was still a woman, with the natural instincts of one. Violence, he had always thought, just wasn't a natural part of a woman's makeup. Or maybe there were some things he didn't know.

Zoe said, "I don't understand about Vincente. I can't see how he could go without even comin' back to bury his wife."

Lanham studied a while. He didn't want everybody to know, but he decided it wouldn't hurt for Zoe to hear. "She's dead, Zoe. Nothin' he could do would bring her back. So he crossed the river. He went over to hunt down bandits and send them after her, one at a time."

Her shoulder was against him, and he felt her shiver. But when he looked, she was smiling grimly. "I hope he gets them. Every last one of them."

"The odds are against that."

"You said you-all got one today."

"Vincente did, really. And your old daddy. This one had been wounded, and the others had left him." He started to tell her all of it, but he decided to leave out the part about Galindo. The mood she was in, not much telling what she might take it into her head to do. "He was hidin' in a pear patch. Vincente got him."

The beef wasn't really done when he took it off of the spits, but the outside was cooked, and in the moonlight they couldn't see the rare blood red of the inside. What they didn't see couldn't make them sick, Lanham figured. Hungry as he was, it tasted fine. They ate their fill and then sat side by side, watching the fire die away to coals.

"It's a hard country, Lanham."

"I wonder if it's worth what it costs."

"Land has always had to be bought with blood, Dad said. There's been too much blood invested here now for me to do anything but stay." She mused. "How long do you think we'll have to put up with border wars and bandits? With havin' to look over our shoulders like frightened deer everywhere we go?"

"Right now I don't know who's big enough to stop it."

"We got us a sheriff."

"He's been in office since before the big war. Maybe he's gettin' a little tired. Anyway, there's more territory than he can cover, him and a few deputies."

"There's the United States army at Fort Brown."

"Yellow-leg Yankee officers that don't understand the country and don't care if they never do. They're just waitin' for a transfer to somethin' better. And mostly they got Negro troops that come from all over the South and are like a fish out of water in a place like this. They joined the army because they was hungry—most of them—not because they wanted to be soldiers. Every time a patrol goes out to scout the river, the word moves ahead of them. The bandits know where they're goin', how long it'll take them to get there, and how long they'll be gettin' back. All they got to do is cross over behind the troops, raid till they've had a bellyful, and cross back."

"Dad heard a rumor McNelly is fixin' to bring the Rangers."

Lanham snorted. "McNelly!"

"Did you ever see him?"

"No, but I seen a-plenty of them carpetbag State Police, before the people got their vote back and throwed them out. I got no confidence in any man who was ever connected with that outfit."

"He might be different."

"Why? And even if he wasn't counterfeit, he'll still be hamstrung by the same laws that hold the sheriff down, and the army. Anybody they catch, they got to take to town. The bandits get out on bail, and they high-tail it across the river. Or they leave what they stole and nobody can prove they had it. Not one of them ever gets hung. Not one of them ever stays in jail long enough to get tired of the cookin'."

Zoe pondered darkly. "Then it's up to us, isn't it?"

"How do you mean?"

"If the bandits can spit on the law, then we'll have to say to hell with the law, too. We'll have to do what they do, make our own law." She leaned against him. Her hand sought and found his hand. "You'll help me, won't you, Lanham? You'll stay with me?"

He couldn't have said no if he had wanted to. "I'll stay, Zoe."

She leaned against him harder, her forehead against his cheek. Surprised, he put his arms around Zoe and held her. She was a strong woman, but not so much so that she didn't need the comfort of a man's strength. She was a woman suddenly alone, in grief and shock. It occurred to Lanham that she was in an emotional mood now that he could take advantage of, if he were that way inclined. He had a strong feeling she would offer little resistance to anything he might want to do.

Many a night he had lain on his bedroll and wished for her. Now he had her. But the time was wrong, the situation was wrong. Old Griffin Daingerfield still lay yonder unburied.

Some things a man just didn't do.

Six

A WHILE AFTER DAYLIGHT, A BAILEY ranch *vaquero* came by, and Lanham gave the startled rider a message to take to his *patrón*. Well after that, they heard many horses. Lanham grabbed his rifle and signaled Zoe to run for the chaparral. He followed her, looking back. They knelt in the brush and watched cautiously. Lanham knew it was probably help arriving, but he didn't care to stake his life on it. He kept his eyes on the heavy-set rider who spurred out in the lead. He thought he knew, but he waited until certain recognition came.

"It's all right, Zoe. That's Bonifacio."

They stood up together and walked out into the ranch yard. The graying sheriff reined up in front of them. He took a long, grim look at the ruins about him and finally eased his tired body to the ground, stretching his legs. It had been a long night, and he wasn't a young man anymore. He held his hat in his hand. "You all right, Miss Daingerfield?"

"I'll *be* all right, Sheriff. Glad you came."

Sheriff Brown went through the amenities, expressing his regret for the death of Griffin Daingerfield. While he talked, Lanham shook hands with Bonifacio and looked over the faces of the twenty or so men who had come with the sheriff. Most were strangers to him. The majority were Anglos, but a handful were Mexican. The struggle along the border was not altogether on racial lines.

The sheriff said, "I've got a wagon on the way. We can take your father to town."

Zoe replied, "He's not going to town. I want to bury him here."

She received no argument from the sheriff, but she went on, "This was his ranch. He lived for it; he died for it. Here is where he stays."

"And the others, the Mexicans?"

"They were part of this place, too. They died with my father."

The sheriff shrugged. "Your choice, ma'am. We'll put a burial crew to work." He looked around somberly. "I thought we'd need the wagon to help you carry your things to town. But it don't look like they left you anything to carry."

"I'm not goin' to town, Sheriff."

The lawman's voice firmed. "Young lady, I expect *I've* got something to say about that."

Lanham saw Zoe's jaw take a hard set. She wasn't just Zoe anymore; she was a part of old Griffin Daingerfield. "This land belongs to the Daingerfields. It belonged to my mother and father. She died, and then it belonged to my father. He died, and I'm the only Daingerfield left. It belongs to me. Now, damn them, the only way they're goin' to get me off of this land is to put me *under* it."

The sheriff tried argument, but it was like running up against an abode wall four feet thick. His face darkened, and he turned away to pace up and down the yard. He came back to try again, and the wall still stood.

"I'm stayin'," Zoe said.

The sheriff's jaw chewed, though he had nothing to chew on. "Well, we got other things to do right now. We'll talk about it some more."

"*You* talk about it, Sheriff," Zoe said. "I've had my say."

Brown gave up trying to reason with Zoe. He set in to questioning Lanham. He said he knew it was useless to try to trail the cattle now. It always was by the time a posse could get to the scene.

Lanham said, "They crossed before dark yesterday. We was there just afterward, me and Vincente de Zavala."

The sheriff's eyes narrowed. "This Vincente . . . I haven't seen him. Where's he at?"

Lanham frowned. "He's not here."

"That's his wife they killed, isn't it? He's got to be here."

"He's not."

"Where did he go?"

Lanham's face twisted. He had told Zoe, but he didn't think he should tell anybody else. News had a way of traveling across that river like it had been sent by telegraph. "He killed a man yesterday. He was afraid to come back."

"Who did he kill?"

"We caught up to one *bandido*. He was wounded. Vincente . . . well, you can imagine the way he felt about his wife. The bandit shot at me, and Vincente was defendin' me the first couple of shots. After that . . . he kept shootin' that *hombre* till . . ." Lanham grimaced. "It wasn't a pretty sight. He got scared then. Lit out."

"I don't see what he had to be scared about. If it was up to me, I'd give him a medal."

"Wasn't you he was worried about, Sheriff. Them boys across the river, they got a short fuse and a long memory. Remember old Jesús Sandoval? Bandits killed his wife and daughter, and then he killed some of *them*. He's been sleepin' in the brush ever since, on the dodge. Can't even go to his own place without company, or they'd get him. Vincente figured it'd be that way with him, too, so he lit out north, toward San Antone."

The story sounded plausible enough. If he hadn't known it to be a lie, he would have believed it himself. It satisfied the sheriff.

One of the possemen carried a Bible in his saddlebags, just over his rifle. He was a drifting minister of sorts, working in the fields and on the ranges for sustenance, preaching wherever the faithful would pause to listen. He told of the man Griffin Daingerfield and the mighty rock he had been. He extolled the faithfulness of Hilario Gomez and the tender innocence of the young wife María, cruelly taken from this life before she could deliver her first-born into the world to insure her immortality here. He held the Bible open but did not look at it. He quoted it from memory, his eyes closed, and finished with a prayer that was half supplication, half anger: "Oh, Lord, please receive these good people to Thy bosom and show them of Thy mercy, and deliver into our hands those heathen ones who have put them here, and we shall show them no mercy whatever. Amen."

Lanham led Zoe away from the burying. Her shoulders quivered a little, but no audible sound escaped her. The more he looked at her, the more he saw of Griffin Daingerfield in her eyes, her strong mouth. "It'll be all right, Zoe. Maybe you ought to listen to the sheriff and go to Brownsville with him. I'll stay here and watch after things."

"Don't make me have to fight you, too, Lanham."

He had no intention of doing that. He knew that if she didn't want to go, the only way they could take her would be to put the handcuffs on and drag her. And they would have to fight *him* first.

He heard horses' hoofs drumming in the brush. Turning, he saw dust rising in the west. Half a dozen riders burst into the clearing and trotted their horses across the yard. Andrew Bailey, a neighbor, swung down from a big sorrel and handed the reins to one of his *vaqueros*. He swept his hat from his head in a grand gesture and bowed in a manner that went back far beyond the Confederacy. "Zoe, I got here as soon as I could. I wish I'd known sooner. I wish I'd been here when it happened. It might not have ended this way."

He extended his hands, and Zoe took them. Lanham watched the ranchman narrow-eyed. It wasn't that he had any reason to distrust him; it was just that it had seemed to him that Bailey used to come over here more often than simple neighborliness called for. After all, he had a good-sized ranch of his own, and it had seemed to Lanham that a man with that much country to see after wouldn't have time to go calling so regularly. He had a wife, too. A Mexican wife. Rumor was that he had married her some years ago because she had inherited some land he wanted. Be that as it may, she was his wife. The fact that he was married was probably why old Griffin never regarded Bailey as one of Zoe's suitors, and why he never ran him off the way he did the others who came to campaign for his daughter. An old sinner in some respects, Griffin had never strayed from *his* wife and wouldn't have thought of it. Probably he never thought it likely that a man of Andrew Bailey's stature would do it, either.

That was one of Griffin's notions Lanham Neal had never shared.

Bailey was a large man of about forty or so, with a square, sun-browned face that Lanham conceded probably would look handsome to a woman; he wouldn't argue that point one way or the other. Bailey was beginning to show a touch of frost at the temples, but anyone who took that for a sign of weakness just wasn't paying attention. Bailey had been tough enough to make a go of the cow business in a country where the weak couldn't stay. He had fought outlaws off of his place more than once, sending them high-tailing it for the river. No one denied his strength or his nerve.

"Zoe," Bailey said, "anything I have that you need, just ask for it. You can come and stay with us for as long as you want to."

"Thank you, Andrew, but I've already fought that out with Lanham and the sheriff. I'm stayin' right here."

"Anything you need, then . . . food, clothes, some men to help you rebuild your house."

"Some food, some clothes . . . I'd appreciate that, Andrew. As for a house, it takes money to buy and haul lumber. What little money I have, I'll need to fight with. If you can send some men to help us build three or four *jacales*, I'll be much obliged."

"Zoe, you're a white woman. You can't live in a *jacal* like some Mexican."

"I did once, when I was little. It was good enough for my mother. I think I can be as tough as she was. I'm holdin' onto the land first. There'll be time enough someday for a house."

Bailey's big hands crushed his hatbrim, and his eyes were dark with concern. "I'll not argue the point with you, Zoe, if you've done made up your mind. But I ought to point out a few facts. You're awful close to the river here. A dozen men wouldn't be protection enough if the *Cortinistas* came again in strength. Beyond that, you're a woman, a good-lookin' *young* woman. You belong in Brownsville, with a good house and pretty clothes and the comforts of town . . . not out here in a mud-and-brush shack with dirt in your hair and watchin' all the time for Cheno Cortina's men."

"Andrew . . ."

"Hear me out, Zoe. You could go to Brownsville. I could run this place for you and split the profit. If there was fightin' to be done, you wouldn't be in no danger. The ranch could pay you and you could live the way a woman like you is intended to."

Lanham still frowned. He knew where *he* would be if Bailey took over. Out. It struck him, too, that Bailey would have to go to town every so often to report to Zoe. Lanham doubted he would take his wife along. Bailey hadn't brought her here the last couple or three years, not since Zoe had blossomed out.

The sheriff listened hopefully. "Andrew's talkin' sense, Miss Daingerfield. You sure ought to listen to him."

Even Lanham would admit it was a logical answer, except for the part about Bailey going to town so often.

But Zoe turned it down, as Lanham had known she would. "Thank you, Andrew. I appreciate you bein' so concerned. It's good to have friends. But I already told you how it's goin' to be."

Bailey said, "Runnin' a ranch ain't for a woman. You'll need help."

Lanham put in firmly, "She's got help."

Bailey stared at him, and Lanham didn't see any good will. *Probably wishing I was the one had the Mexican wife.*

The wagon came, finally. As it had turned out, its trip was largely wasted. Not entirely, however, for someone had thoughtfully put blankets in it, expecting to haul back Zoe Daingerfield, and perhaps her father. The blankets would come in handy. They had also put in tin cups and a pot and some home-parched coffee. The possemen made good use of that while they rested for the long ride back to Brownsville.

Bonifacio sadly poked through the ruins in a vain search for anything useful he could salvage. He came trudging back empty-handed and slump-shouldered.

Lanham peered at him across a coffee cup. "Bonifacio, I'll need to find some extra help for Zoe. You'll stay, won't you?"

Bonifacio shook his head. "This is a bad place now. The saints will forever shrink from it."

"We're not saints, Bonifacio."

"Those *ladrones* will be back. They will keep coming so long as there are *gringo* cattle to take and *gringo* blood to spill. I do not want them to spill any of mine."

Disappointed, Lanham accepted Bonifacio's decision. "We'll miss you, *amigo*."

"You should leave, too, *caporál*. You should leave and take *la patrona* with you. That Cheno, he has eyes watching all the time. He will know you have stayed. He will know how many are here, and where they are when he wants to strike. Like they knew yesterday."

Suspicion touched Lanham. "You're tryin' to say somethin', Bonifacio. Put it into words."

"I have a family in Matamoros. Cortina, he will send someone to slit their throats. . . ."

Andrew Bailey took a long step forward. "If you're holding something back, *hombre*, I'll slit *yours*."

Lanham moved between Bailey and Bonifacio. "He won't. But then, *I* might. Out with it, *amigo*." Bonifacio stared at the ground, trembling. Lanham said, "We been friends. As your friend, I'm askin' you to tell if there's somethin' we ought to know."

Eyes afraid, the chubby *vaquero* shrugged. "Tomorrow I will wish I had not spoken. But I will tell you. Yesterday, when I rode for the sheriff, my horse was tired. I thought to myself, 'I will stop at the *rancho* of my friend Ezequiel Archuleta and borrow a fresh horse.' So I stopped, and I started to tell Ezequiel and his brother Rodrigo what had happened. But they already knew. They told me they were glad I was not here to share what happened to the *gringo patrón*. I asked them how they knew this, and they said they were here. They watched us ride out to hunt for the cattle. The *bandidos* were waiting, hiding. The Archuletas, they went and told them the *patrón* was alone, just him and the old man and Vincente's woman. They said they regretted about the woman. That was not part of the plan. But some of the men from across the river had been into the *tequila*. . . ."

Lanham's fists were clenched so tightly that his fingernails cut into the flesh. Andrew Bailey's square jaw jutted. Zoe's eyes were half closed, but Lanham could see the hard anger building in them. Lanham's fists loosened, then clenched again. He glanced at the sheriff, and then at the possemen. "Sheriff, I'm fixin' to go pay a call to them Archuletas. Anybody wants to go with me is sure welcome."

The sheriff's worry was plain. "Now, boy, we got to be legal. Let's talk this over a little bit."

"We'll talk it over when we've finished."

Zoe Daingerfield clutched Lanham's arm. "Thank you, Lanham." Her eyes met the sheriff's. "It'll be done by law, Sheriff. Cheno Cortina's law. Let's go, Lanham."

Lanham said, "Not you, Zoe."

But she was already going after her horse. Lanham caught Bailey looking at him with a touch of resentment. Lanham suspected Bailey, too, had been about to propose a ride to Archuleta's. Lanham had beaten him to it. Bailey said, "Better stop her. She's got no business there."

"You'd have to chain her to a mesquite to stop her if she really intends to go. And it looks like she does."

Seven

THE POSSEMEN GRABBED THEIR HORSES
and swung into the saddle. The sheriff tried to get up
ahead of them, to gain control. Lanham spurred into the
lead and held it. Andrew Bailey was just behind him,
the possemen stringing out. The sheriff made his way
up, finally, but Lanham could sense that the posse was
following him and Zoe, not Sheriff Brown.

It was ten miles across cactus and mesquite and chaparral to the small cattle and corn-patch place that belonged to the Archuletas. The possemen were tired, for
it had been a long night, but they pushed, keeping close
to the stolid Lanham Neal and the girl with proud shoulders and angry chin.

Spotted, longhorned cows trotted away at the riders'
approach. By habit, Lanham looked for brands or ear-
marks, for perhaps the confident Archuletas had drifted
some of the Slash D cattle over here onto their country,

figuring the death of Griffin made it open season on Daingerfield stock.

The last three miles it seemed to Lanham they ought to come in sight of the Archuleta *jacales* past every draw, every prickly pear patch. It was typical of these brush-country *ranchos*, whether *gringo*-owned or Mexican . . . you never had much sign that you were approaching one. You rode through a thicket and all of a sudden it would lie there in front of you. The Mexican places, especially, looked almost like part of the land, for they were made of materials found close at hand . . . the long, savage spines of ocotillo lined up and tied in tight rows to serve as corrals that not even a *javalina* hog would poke its snout through, the houses themselves made of brush and mud. These places invariably seemed to have risen up out of the ground. They would sink right back into it, soon leaving no trace, if they were ever long abandoned, for there was little or nothing about them alien to the land. For perhaps a couple of hundred years now, Mexicans had roamed up and down this river country between the Nueces and the Bravo, living a while here, a while there. When they left, the hot sun and the warm wind out of Mexico would combine with the infrequent rains to work on what little remained behind, so that in a few years no man would see any sign that anyone had ever been here. Always the land reverted to the lizards and the snakes and the armadillos, the jackrabbits and the *paisano* birds the Anglos called roadrunners.

Zoe Daingerfield's eyes were perhaps sharpened by her hatred. She pointed and gave a shout. "Yonder they are."

Two horsemen had ridden out of an opening in the brush and reined up in surprise at sight of the posse.

Lanham glanced at Bonifacio. Reluctantly the *vaquero* nodded. "Ezequiel and Rodrigo."

The Mexicans' faces were hidden in shadow beneath the brims of peaked sombreros, but Lanham had no doubt that Bonifacio was right. In brush country a man often caught no more than a quick glimpse of a rider. He learned to recognize people by the way they sat in their saddles, the shape they made a-horseback. The Archuletas waited uncertainly, reins drawn tight in their hands, ready to ride forward or whip back in an instant.

Somebody fired a long shot that kicked up dust in front of them. The pair whirled their horses back into the brush.

Lanham raised his voice. "Let's git 'em!"

The sheriff hadn't spoken. He never got to. Lanham's arm came up and over in an arc, and he reached down for his rifle. Spurs jingled and horses grunted with the sudden effort of moving into a lope. Saddle guns slapped against leather as they came up out of long scabbards. Somebody gave a Rebel yell, and the posse hit the brush full tilt. Branches whipped and snapped, and men cursed against the painful grab of thorns, but no one pulled on the reins. Horses instinctively sought the easiest way through and riders gave them their heads, for brush country horses handled this best when left alone. Riders trained to the country ducked, stretched, twisted sideways, avoiding the clutching, tearing spines the best they could. In moments they were in the clear and had a good view of the fugitives just ahead of them, spurring desperately. A posseman fired and missed. From somewhere the Archuletas' horses seemed to reach down and pull up more speed. Across the open flat they ran, stretching their legs in long, land-eating strides.

Lanham glanced back once more and saw that Zoe was keeping up with the main body of men, her face flushed. Some of the possemen yelped and shouted like cowboys out to rope a pair of wolves. Now and then one of them fired, though shots from a running horse could as well be fired by a blind man for all the chance they had of finding their target.

The posse horses were far from fresh, but they gained steadily, most of them. The Archuleta horses, probably fresher, were nevertheless the small Mexican kind. They had an endurance that could carry a man across the river and halfway to Saltillo, but not in a hurry. Speed was not their long suit.

Andrew Bailey drew first blood. He pulled his horse to a stop, jumped off, dropped to one knee, took deliberate aim down the barrel of his rifle and fired. One of the Mexican mounts fell. The rider rolled in the grass and jumped up limping, looking back in desperation. The older brother stopped, whirled about and reached down for him. The downed Mexican swung himself behind the cantle, and the two men were running again.

Lanham saw Andrew Bailey look at Zoe with a grim smile of satisfaction. *He scored that one on me.*

Two men on a horse. *They can't get far now.* Lanham rode full speed, the warm wind whipping his face. Behind him he could hear the sheriff trying to give orders. He couldn't hear the words, and he doubted many others could. They were following Lanham, and they would follow him till the hands had all been dealt.

The gap was narrow. The Mexican behind the saddle held onto his brother with one arm and twisted around with a pistol. He fired several times. His aim was as hopeless as that of the posse, but it gave Lanham a sick feeling every time he saw the pistol flash. There was always a million-to-one chance Archuleta might score a hit. It might get Lanham. Or it might get Zoe.

More brush lay ahead. Lanham knew it was important they stop the Archuletas before they get that far. He decided to do what Bailey had done. He slid his horse to a stop, jumped down, brought the rifle into line and fired.

The Mexican behind the saddle stiffened and began to slip off. The brother tried vainly to hold him. Swinging back onto his horse, Lanham saw the brother grab at the wounded one's shirt, but it tore in his hands. The wounded man bobbed a moment, half on and half off. The brother was looking around in panic.

To the left ran a gully, a deep scar washed in the soft earth by runoff from the rains. He turned the horse to it. The shirt split, and the wounded man fell to the ground. The brother pulled a rifle from a scabbard, jumped out of the saddle and let the horse go. He grabbed the wounded man's arm and pulled him toward the gully. Bullets kicked up dirt around him, but he didn't cut and run. He kept dragging.

Lanham held his fire, letting others do the useless shooting. He brought the rifle up and spurred headlong for the Mexicans like the lead hound closing on a fox. The man on his feet saw Lanham coming and swung his rifle around. Lanham saw the flash and felt the sting of the bullet across his cheek. Almost point-blank, Lanham fired and swept past, giving his attention to the reins to keep from riding full speed off into the gully.

The Mexican staggered, hard hit. He tried to bring up the rifle again, but a bullet from Bailey's rifle struck him, and then someone else's. A dozen shots seemed to be fired all at the same time. The Mexican fell, his body jerking from the impact of bullets, dust flying from his dirty cotton shirt.

Lanham brought his horse around and came back. The possemen were circling the downed Archuletas. One of the pair moved an arm, and half a dozen guns blasted him.

Lanham rubbed a hand across his burning cheek and brought it away bloody. With his fingertips he traced the line the bullet had creased. Not deep enough to amount to anything, but it could leave a faint scar he would be explaining the rest of his life.

Zoe Daingerfield sat on her horse, looking down at the two dead men, her cheeks red, her eyes wide and wild. Her mouth cut into a grim smile.

Lanham felt a sudden dismay, for he didn't like what he saw in her face. The sight of the crumpled Archuletas was enough to make a man a little sick to his stomach. In fact, Lanham was. But if Zoe felt any revulsion, it didn't show. On the contrary, she seemed to be glorying in it.

She raised her eyes to Lanham, finally, and gasped. "Lanham, you're shot." He shook his head quickly. "A scratch, that's all."

She rode to him and leaned forward, putting her hand to his face, anxiously checking the shallow wound. Andrew Bailey watched them, frustration in his eyes. *Probably wishing it had been him that got the scratch instead of me,* Lanham thought. *And I'd as soon it was.*

Zoe said, "I'm sorry, Lanham. I didn't mean for you to be hurt on my account."

A sober thought ran through his mind. *I think maybe she's hurt a lot worse than I am.*

The sheriff looked down at the Archuletas, his face creased with regret. Andrew Bailey told him, "The boys done a real good job. Here's the best two Mexicans you'll see all day."

The sheriff grimaced. "I'd sooner have taken them alive."

"What for? So their friends could get them out of jail?"

"I was thinkin' they might've told us some things if you-all hadn't been so quick-triggered." He glanced accusingly at Lanham, then back at Bailey.

Bailey said, "They'd have told you a bunch of lies, is

all. Now we don't have to worry whether the bail is high
enough, or the jail is strong enough, or the judge is strict
enough. With these two, the jury has already come in.
And there's no appeal."

Bonifacio Holguín had held back, loping along behind
the possemen, staying in sight but taking no part in the
chase. Now he came up hesitantly, his eyes betraying his
fear. Lanham thought he knew what was working on the
vaquero. Bonifacio was certain he was in bad grace for
having tried to withhold information. Beyond that, he
was a Mexican, and right now almost any Mexican was
apt to be suspect.

Zoe Daingerfield's voice was sharp. "Bonifacio!"

The *vaquero* turned his eyes from the dead men. "*Sí,
patrona.*"

She beckoned him to one side, where no one would
hear except Lanham. "You're not leavin' me, Bonifacio.
You'll keep right on workin' for me." Her voice was
commanding. "You know this country on both sides of
the river. You know the people. You'll tell everybody
you've quit me, but you'll go down there and keep your
eyes and ears open and let me know who-all is mixed
up in these raids, you understand? You're goin' to let
me know who they are if they're on this side and when
they're comin' back if they're on the other. Savvy?"

Bonifacio's eyes pleaded. "*Patrona* . . ."

"I'll pay you."

"It is not the pay . . ."

"You'll do it, Bonifacio. You'll do it because you were
always hound-dog scared of my old daddy, and now
you're fixin' to be even scarder of *me*. You'll do it because you know if you don't I'll somehow, someday, get
my hands on you. You know that if I live long enough
I'll take you out to a handy tree and present you with
six feet of rope." Her eyes were narrow and dangerous.
"And if I die first, I'll come back in the spirit and put a

curse on you and dog your steps till you'll beg the devil himself to take you."

Superstition and fear of bad spirits was strong in many of the border people. Zoe knew it. Bonifacio wept silently, his eyes filling with tears. "*Sí, patrona*, whatever you tell me, I will do it."

Kneeling, the sheriff went through the pockets of the dead men while a couple of his possemen picked up their weapons. The sheriff pushed to his feet. From his hand, a pocket watch dangled on a chain. "You'll want this, Miss Daingerfield."

Lanham leaned forward. He recognized the watch. There was no counting the times he had seen Griffin Daingerfield take it from his pocket and glance at it confidently, then look up as if he were checking on the accuracy of the sun.

Zoe clasped the watch so hard her knuckles went white.

Bonifacio had gone to Brownsville with the sheriff and the posse. Andrew Bailey had returned to his ranch with his *vaqueros*, promising to find Zoe some trustworthy help and send it as quickly as he could. He had left regretfully, for when he was gone there had been only Zoe and Lanham left at the ruins of the Daingerfield place . . . the two of them, alone.

The sheriff's wagon had left the coffee and the pot behind, and the blankets. Lanham cut some more beef off the hindquarter and set it to broil on the mesquite-limb spits while coffee simmered in the pot. Zoe sat across the fire from him, withdrawn into herself. She hadn't spoken since Bailey had left. Her face was still flushed. Her eyes had a faraway involvement with whatever images were running through her mind. She wasn't here with Lanham, not in spirit, anyway.

He was sure the excitement of the chase still ran high

in her. The sight of blood had affected her like whisky, and she was still a little drunk on it.

She ate the beef and drank her coffee, staring silently at him. *Maybe she's finally coming back*, he thought.

Darkness fell as they finished eating. He glanced at the blankets. "Zoe, I been thinkin' about what Bonifacio said. If the Archuletas were spyin' on us for Cortina's men, somebody else might be, too. It'd be easy for them to slip in here during the night and get us both. I think maybe we better not stay here, not till we've got some help."

She spoke the first words she had said in a couple of hours. "What do you think we ought to do?"

"After it gets dark we ought to slip off somewhere, out into the brush where they can't find us."

She nodded. "All right."

With darkness he quietly saddled the horses, tied the blankets on behind the saddles and gave Zoe a boost up. They rode in silence a couple of miles. He dismounted and helped her to the ground, then took the saddles off and staked the horses.

"They'd have to bring dogs to find us now," he said.

He spread a couple of blankets beneath a mesquite. "This is for you." He turned away, another blanket under his arm, to find a place for himself.

Zoe caught his hand and turned him around. "Lanham . . ." Her eyes were warm. Her blood was still up. "Lanham, I want to thank you for what you did today . . . for me . . . for my father."

"Zoe, you don't have to . . ."

Her fingers touched his cheek. It was sore now, and the fingers brought pain, but he did not pull away or flinch. "Lanham, I'll never forget that you got this fighting for me."

Her fingers moved on past his cheek and around to the back of his neck, pulling his head down. She raised up on her toes to meet his mouth with her own. He was surprised at the warmth of her face, like she had a fever or something. Her other hand went around him and pulled him against her with an insistence he had never dared wish for. She kissed the wounded cheek, then kissed his mouth again, her breathing warm and rapid.

"Lanham, I want you to stay with me. I don't want you to leave me, not for a minute."

Last night had been the wrong time and the wrong place, and he had told himself there were some things a man just didn't do. Now he couldn't think of any reasons. He could only think of Zoe, of the need she had for him, and he had for her. He kissed her hungrily, the way he had wanted to since the first time he had ridden up to the Daingerfield place and had seen her standing on the gallery of the big house, her full skirt billowing, her long hair flowing in the wind. He dropped the blanket from under his arm and sank with her to the one beneath his feet.

She ran her fingers through his hair. There was something wild and violent in her eyes that might have scared him had he been calm enough to see it as it really was. "Promise me you'll stay with me, Lanham. Promise me you'll help me hunt them down and kill them—every last one of them—the way we did those two today."

He crushed her in his arms, ready to promise her anything. "I will, Zoe. You know I will."

Eight

TWO BODIES DANGLED FROM HEAVY limbs of a huge old live-oak tree. They twisted slowly, the Gulf breeze catching the tatters of their poor clothing and fluttering them like forlorn flags. Mexicans, both.

Captain McNelly stared awhile in silence, his jaw set hard, his beard seeming to bristle. "Sergeant, I see some people sitting yonder in the edge of that thicket."

"Families, sir. They've been afraid to cut these men down."

"Families? Then these men didn't come from Mexico. They're natives." McNelly's gaze turned to a local man who had come along with the Rangers as a guide.

The man twisted in his saddle, nervous. "Not all the bandits come from across the river, Captain. Sometimes they have help on this side."

"It wasn't bandits who hung these men. It was one of these local posses, wasn't it?"

The guide looked at the ground. "I wasn't here, Captain. I can't tell you none of the details."

"Then tell me what you *do* know."

"Well, sir, them *bandidos*, they hit Jim Sm . . . they hit one of the ranches here day before yesterday; run off with some mighty good horses. Some of the boys got together and went lookin' for them."

"And when they didn't catch up with the renegades, they chose to hang some local Mexicans instead."

The guide shrugged. "With Mexicans, it's hard to tell who's your friend and who ain't."

"So when in doubt, you just string them up."

"Like I say, Captain, I didn't do it. I wasn't here."

"You know those men hanging there?"

"Yes, sir. They're a couple Mexicans been givin' old . . . one of the ranchers some trouble over a piece of land they claim is theirs. *Claimed.*"

The big sergeant nodded darkly. "It's a good thing for some folks that there's a bandit raid every now and again. Gives them an excuse to get rid of a few people they don't like."

The captain eased to the ground, overtaken by a sudden fit of coughing. It racked him mercilessly. Some of the new recruits watched in dismay, but the older Rangers found interests elsewhere and acted as if they didn't see it happen. When the coughing was over, the captain glanced at his handkerchief, grimaced and wadded it back into his pocket so no one could see it. He leaned against his horse, gathering his strength. "Sergeant, I want you to detail a couple of men to cut those bodies down. You ride over and tell those people in the thicket to come and claim their kin."

Hesitantly the guide cleared his throat. "Captain, some of the local boys ain't goin' to cotton to that much. When they hang a man, they want him to dangle there.

Lesson to the others. That's why those people yonder been afraid to come and cut the bodies down theirselves."

The captain's quiet voice crackled like fire running through dry saltgrass. "I don't give a tinker's damn what the local boys don't like. I wasn't sent down here to be popular; I was sent to bring law and order to the Nueces Strip. I was sent to bring peace, and I'll bring it if I have to personally shoot, hang or club to death half the male population—Mexican *and gringo*. At least when I leave here the rest of them will be ready for a spell of quiet."

The man shrugged. "Suits me, Captain. I never had any particular stomach for this kind of business myself. But some think it's necessary."

"It isn't. I'm going to stop it."

"Hope you do, Captain. And if you do, you're a bigger man than you look like."

A rain had drifted across this strip of country, and the ground was soft. The chuckwagon mired now and again. Dad Smith, the cook, was down regularly raking huge gobs of mud off of the light wheels. To save the horses— the going was slow anyway because of the wagon—the captain dismounted, loosened his cinch and started walking, leading. The other men followed his example in military order. The guide muttered something about how he wasn't being paid to ride, much less to walk, but he gave up being the lone holdout after a while and walked with the rest.

Hours later one of the scouts came trotting back. "Big bunch of horsemen comin' our way, Captain. Movin' up from the south."

"Look like bandits?"

"No way to tell, sir. They saw us. Way they're ridin', doesn't look like they intend to try and avoid us."

The captain didn't waste motions, nor did he rush. He tightened the cinch, strapped on the pistol belt he had preferred to loop across his saddlehorn rather than carry, and swung up onto his horse. He didn't have to give an order. The older Rangers watched his example and did whatever he did. The newer Rangers, in turn, went by what they saw. The captain laid his rifle across his saddle, not with any threatening gesture but just so it would be seen and appreciated.

Captain McNelly was not given to unnecessary talk. Most of the time his men watched his face—particularly his eyes—and read there what they really needed to know. For the rest of what they *wanted* to know, they usually did without. The captain was a man who kept his own counsel and did not often bother to explain his reasons. Of his men he expected obedience, not understanding.

"They don't appear to be Mexicans, Sergeant."

"No, sir. There's twenty-five, maybe thirty of them. If they was bandits, they wouldn't ride bold as brass right up to an outfit like this."

The captain chewed his unlighted cigar. "Not *Mexican* bandits, anyway." He ordered the Rangers spread out in a skirmish line. He glanced at the local man. "Know them?"

"Yes, sir. The one in the lead, that's Jim Smith. He's one of them that got up a bunch of men after the raid."

Captain's narrowed eyes focused on the leader, a tall, tired-looking man with a week's growth of whiskers and a slump that told of hard days in the saddle. As he came within hailing distance of the Rangers, Smith raised his hand to signal his men to slow from a trot to a walk. He edged up a length or two ahead of his lieutenants. He made a half-military salute that indicated he had seen service. "Howdy, Cap. I expect you'd be McNelly?" He had a deep Southern accent. Georgia, maybe.

The captain's tone was icy. "And what makes you expect that?"

"Word's been out that you was a-comin' soon's you could get you enough men recruited. Nobody knowed just when." He turned in the saddle and swept his arm back to show off his men. "This is our vigilance committee. We're all mighty glad you made it, Cap. We're ready to throw in and help you. Just tell us what to do."

Captain chewed on the cold cigar, his eyes still narrow as he slowly assessed the caliber of the posse. The assessment done, he scowled. "What you'll do is go home."

"Home?" The posse leader pushed himself back in the saddle. "Cap, I don't think you understand how things are down thisaway."

"I understand how things are, and you'd better understand how they're *going* to be. I said you'll go home; I *meant* you'll go home. What's more, you'll stay there!"

Smith colored. "Now looky here, McNelly . . ."

"No, *you* look. In the first place, I'm not *Cap*, and I'm not McNelly. I'm *Captain* McNelly. You'll do well to remember that. In the second place, I want this committee disbanded, and I want you men to go to your homes. There'll be no more of these freelance posses out. If you're the leader of this bunch, you'll give your men that order."

Smith shifted his weight in the saddle. He was a tall man on a big horse, and for that reason he looked down on McNelly a little. He was plainly one who didn't take kindly to orders from anyone he had to look down upon. "I don't know as they'd want to do that."

"It's of no concern to me what any of you want. You disband them or I will."

"You got no authority . . ."

"I *do* have the authority, given me by the governor of the state of Texas to stop all armed and lawless bands of men. That means Mexicans . . . it means Americans . . . it means anybody who goes out in armed groups unless they're under my command. It means you, Smith."

Smith stared sullenly, measuring this little man with his eyes, still unconvinced.

McNelly added, "I have full authority to kill. In fact, I was *ordered* to kill anyone who resists. If you know anything about me, Smith, you know I follow orders. If you *don't* know anything about me, then you may be just about to find out. I'm giving your band ten minutes to break up and go your separate ways. After ten minutes, you'll all be considered a mob, and these Rangers have my orders to shoot." He paused. "If you don't think Rangers will follow orders, then you don't know much about them, either."

Captain raised his rifle a little. Behind him, leather squeaked as Rangers brought pistols and rifles to the ready.

Smith's eyes widened, following the flurry of movement. His gaze cut back to McNelly, and for a few moments he tried to stare the captain down. But McNelly's eyes were steady as a rock, and as hard. The guide nervously began edging away from what might become the line of fire. Smith's chin dropped. He cut his eyes away, cursing softly beneath his breath. He turned his horse around.

One of Smith's lieutenants rode up to McNelly and hesitantly extended his pistol, holding it by the barrel. "You want to take our guns, Captain?"

McNelly might have relaxed then, but he didn't. "No, keep them. You may need them for defense. But *only* for defense. There'll be no more of this useless hanging or shooting of men just because you don't happen to like them. From now on any such act will be considered murder. I've already told you what my orders are. You'd better make up your minds that I'll carry them out."

The rider said, "Captain, I'll never doubt anything I ever hear about you."

McNelly sat in the saddle and watched as the possemen rode by him. A few peeled off and headed east or west or south. Most lived to the north, and they rode that way. But they didn't ride as a group. They made it a point to break up into pairs or threes. Smith was the last to go. He watched in sullen silence. As he started to leave, McNelly called to him once more. "Smith, you'd better remember. If there's any killing to be done, I'll do it. Don't make me come hunting for you."

Smith didn't even look at him. He just touched spurs to his horse and rode off.

Slowly the Rangers reholstered their pistols and slipped their rifles back into the scabbards beneath their legs. McNelly gave no orders. He simply started riding again, south.

The guide reined in beside the sergeant. His hands still trembled a little as he looked ahead toward the captain. "Sergeant, if it had come to a showdown, would he have really done it?"

The sergeant's eyes gleamed. "What do *you* think?"

Nine

LANHAM NEAL HAD AN IDEA ANDREW
Bailey was just making big talk to impress Zoe, promising so much help. He was wrong. The day after the Archuleta shooting, Bailey brought a wagon, its bed filled with supplies. He wasted hardly a look at Lanham. He swept his hat from his gray-templed head and bowed toward Zoe Daingerfield.

"Zoe, this wagon is yours as long as you need it. I hope you'll use it to carry you to Brownsville, where it's safe."

Zoe Daingerfield came near smiling. "We ... I appreciate you bein' so generous, Andrew. And I *will* use it to go to Brownsville. But not to stay ... to bring back more things we'll need."

Bailey's eyes cut to Lanham. "Neal, don't you talk her into any foolish notions."

"Not me. I figure like you ... she ought to go to Brownsville and stay there. But she's a grown woman."

Bailey frowned, looking back at Zoe. "Yes, that she is. She surely is." He studied her, and the look in his eyes was not entirely solicitude. "Then, Zoe, if you won't accept my advice, at least accept my help. Anything I have, all you got to do is ask for it."

Zoe took the offer in good grace. "I'll remember that. But now I'll only ask for the loan of the wagon and team. Tomorrow Lanham and I will go into Brownsville and buy whatever we'll need to get this place halfway back onto its feet. And try to hire some help."

"Be careful who you bring back here," Bailey warned. "Lots of people these days you can't trust." He looked straight at Lanham.

Lanham said evenly, "We'll keep an eye out."

Bailey left them reluctantly, looking over his shoulder. *Suspicious,* Lanham thought. *But what business is she of his? He's already got a wife, Mexican or not. He's tied up tight.*

As before, they slept in the brush away from headquarters, then set out before daylight along the trail to Brownsville. Zoe leaned against him on the wagonseat, but her mind was far away. "Lanham," she said after a while, "besides some help, we've got to build us some kind of a shelter. I was thinkin' . . . there's a Mexican squatter lives down yonderway. Galindo, I think his name is. He'd know how to build a *jacal,* and likely he'd appreciate a few days of paid work. They're always hungry, his kind."

Lanham swallowed, glad she wasn't looking at him. He had made up his mind she shouldn't know about Galindo, for she would probably want to kill him. "Not him, Zoe. You don't want him."

"Why not? He's close by and handy."

"Vincente told me he's got a reputation as a sneak thief. You couldn't afford to take your eyes off of him."

"We got awful little he could steal."

"Just the same, we'd be better off to find us somebody else. We got trouble enough."

Lanham didn't have a coin to his name, but he drew five dollars against Zoe's account at the hotel to get himself a shave, a bath and a clean shirt, and to be able to buy a few drinks for prospective cowboys or *vaqueros*. He ate supper with Zoe and said goodnight to her in the hotel lobby where everybody could observe his leavetaking. "See you in the mornin', Zoe. Maybe by that time I'll have us some help."

She wore new but plain clothes she had bought. She was ill at ease, for she had never spent much time in town. "I wish you would stay here with me."

"You know why I can't. Get a good night's sleep on a good, clean bed. You may not have another for a long time."

He bowed the way Andrew Bailey would and backed away from her, hat in hand. Glancing back as he walked out into the night, he saw her watching him until he passed beyond the lamplight.

Lanham knew the saloons where out-of-work cowboys usually sat around waiting for somebody to come along hiring. He had spent time there. He went to these one by one and announced his need. But the word had come to town with the sheriff and his posse. Everybody knew what had happened out at the Daingerfield place.

One cowboy said, "Sure, I need a job, but not that bad. I hear tell them *bandidos* lost a man or two. They don't like that. They're apt to go back one of these days and really sweep out. If you was hirin' twenty or thirty, where a man'd stand a chance, that'd be different. But four or five . . . we'd be like bait on a hook."

It was the same story everywhere, with variations. Lanham went to the Anglo cowboys first, for he figured they were less likely to have any tie with Cortina. When he ran out of prospects among that crowd, he started on the Mexican *vaqueros*, knowing there was always a chance he would pick up a *Cortinista*. After all, a man couldn't tell by looking.

By midnight, when he gave up, he'd found one *hombre*. This man had said he would bring his brother. Next morning they were waiting patiently at the wagonyard when he opened his eyes and blinked at the rising sun.

"Zoe," he told her at breakfast, "all the luck I've had was bad, pretty near. All I could find was two *hombres*."

"Can we trust them?"

"Can we trust anybody?"

"I guess not."

"Just because we use them don't mean we can't keep an eye on them. Unless we want to stay out there by ourselves, we got to take the chance."

She nodded. "All right. Andrew said he would try to find some help for us, too."

Lanham frowned into his coffee.

He went with Zoe to the bank and stood while she made arrangements for cash and to hold what she could of her father's thin line of credit. The bank, Lanham noted, pulled in considerably when they found out Daingerfield's daughter would be running things. But they couldn't back out altogether; they already had too much invested with the old man. The banker gave Zoe many admonitions with which she readily agreed and with which she would dispense the moment she got out of town.

They loaded the wagon and started down the street to meet the two *vaqueros*. Half a dozen Mexican horsemen came toward them, pulling aside as they neared the wagon. Zoe said, "Look, Lanham, one of them is Bonifacio."

Lanham squinted. "Sure enough, it is. Don't speak to him or stare at him. Don't let on like you know him."

He said regretfully, "These days, it can be worth a Mexican's life to have friends among the *gringos*." Lanham got cold glances from all the riders as they passed by . . . all but Bonifacio. Plain enough where their sympathies lay. Cortina had them convinced.

Bonifacio didn't speak or give any sign of recognition. "Well," Lanham said, "he done what you told him. He fell right in with the crowd. Now let's see if he finds out anything."

The moon was up when they reached the ranch. Lanham rode in alone, using one of the *vaqueros'* horses. After a cautious look around, he brought Zoe. He hadn't felt secure about leaving her with the two strangers, but it would be even riskier to take her into the ranch without a careful reconnaissance.

The first few days, the *vaqueros* did more work afoot than a-horseback, clearing wreckage and building *jacales*. Lanham and the Reyna brothers took pains with the one for Zoe. At best it wouldn't be pretty, but it would keep the rain off. They built a second for Lanham, not far from Zoe's. A third went up for the men, nearer the corrals.

Lanham was careful always to keep either the two men or Zoe in his sight. On the one hand he appreciated the brothers coming out when no one else would. On the other hand he could not help but be a little uneasy about their motives. They turned out to be a genial pair and good help, Reynaldo and Jacinto Reyna. He found himself enjoying their company and feeling guilty about his lingering suspicions.

Damn a country where a man can't even trust the people who help him.

But he never felt so guilty that he let up watching. Nights, he slept uneasily, coming awake at any sound or movement, real or imagined. And he found himself imagining quite a few.

Often when he awakened, he found Zoe lying beside him silent, her eyes wide open.

"What's the matter?" he would ask. "Can't you sleep?"

She would shake her head. "I keep thinkin' of those men across the river, and of my father. I don't think I'll ever sleep right until they're all where *he* is."

In moods like that she turned to Lanham for comfort. His rough cowboy upbringing had not prepared him to give her real tenderness, but he tried. He found little tenderness in Zoe. Always just beneath the surface he sensed violence, a bitterness fighting constantly for release.

He hadn't told the Reyna brothers about Bonifacio Holguín, for if they were spies it could mean Bonifacio's life. So when Bonifacio came in the darkness of night, Lanham had to fling his blanket aside and run hard to keep one of the quick-triggered *vaqueros* from shooting him. The incident, when it was over, eased his mind on one thing. He needn't worry anymore about the loyalty of the Reynas. Bonifacio had narrowly missed having the fourth grave out in the chaparral.

Trembling, Bonifacio said, "I have come to speak to *la patrona*. She is here, *caporál?*"

"She is here."

"Would you wake her?"

"She's awake." He led the wary Mexican to the mud shack. Bonifacio stopped at the door and turned half around, nervously looking back toward the *vaquero* who had come so near to shooting him. "It is safe to talk here?"

Zoe came to the door, a blanket wrapped around her. "It is safe. Come in, Bonifacio."

There were no chairs, except a crude one Jacinto had fashioned of mesquite limbs and green rawhide. Zoe seated herself, carefully keeping her body covered with the blanket. "You have news?"

Bonifacio sat on the dirt floor, sombrero gripped in both big hands. "*Sí patrona*. As you told me, I have traveled much and listened much. But it is very dangerous. They are suspicious, those *ladrones*."

"The news," she said impatiently, "What is it?"

"I know of a raid. Not on this *rancho*, but on some other. Do you know a man named Gaspar Montoya?"

Lanham did. "Small *ranchero*. Got a place west of Bailey's."

"*Sí*. This Montoya, he spies for the bandits. They will cross tomorrow night for certain. And if not tomorrow night, the next night without fail. They will meet this Montoya at his place and he will lead them to a ranch where they expect to take many horses. Perhaps the Bailey ranch; I do not know."

"How many men?"

Bonifacio shrugged. "Who can say? However many feel like it when the time comes to swim the river. Maybe ten, maybe twenty, maybe half a hundred. The word is out for the patriots who want to go."

Zoe trembled with excitement. "Lanham, let's go to Andrew's, now. We'll set a trap at Montoya's. This time they'll pay real good."

Her eagerness troubled him. This wasn't the way a woman was expected to act, not according to Lanham's upbringing. "Easy, Zoe. Tomorrow'll be time enough. We best wait for daylight." He looked at Bonifacio. "You won't be goin' with us. We can't risk havin' you seen."

Bonifacio sighed in relief. "It is better so." He wiped sweat from his face, though the night was cool. "I should go now, and be far from here at daylight. If I could have some coffee . . ."

"Sure, *amigo*. Come on down to my shack and I'll

boil us both some. Zoe, you better get you some sleep."

But he figured she wouldn't sleep anymore tonight. She would lie awake and alone in her blankets on the dirt floor, planning revenge.

Andrew Bailey paced the floor of his parlor like a caged cougar. "How did you come by this information, Zoe?"

She glanced at Lanham, and Lanham answered for her. "Can't tell you. We'd risk a man's life if the word got out."

"Who would *I* tell?" Bailey demanded. "Some damned Mexican?" His Mexican wife sat quietly knitting. Lanham saw her flinch, her lips drawing a little tight. When he saw that Lanham wasn't going to tell him more, Bailey seemed to accept the story he had been brought. He stomped back and forth across the floor, cursing. "Gaspar Montoya! That lousy, pepper-bellied Judas! When the chips are down, you just can't trust a damned Mexican!" He ignored the fact that his wife was listening. She was a plump, olive-skinned woman seated properly in a corner, keeping her place as Mexican women had been taught to do for uncounted generations, being seen discreetly and heard almost never. Lanham figured she might have been a handsome woman once, ten or fifteen years ago, but dark sadness was graven into her face now. He guessed from her form that she took more pleasure in her table than in her husband anymore. She must know better than anyone that to Bailey she was little more than a piece of property, like his horses or his cattle. She bore with Indian-like stoicism the tragedy of rejection and neglect, but the shadows of it lay deep in her eyes.

It was a tragedy shared by many a Mexican woman, married by an Anglo for her property or for her youthful fire and beauty at a time when few Anglo women were available, then set aside like worn-out merchandise in later years as conditions changed . . . treated as a liability, hidden from the world as a symbol of some youthful folly long since regretted, long since renounced.

She ought to take a sharp knife to him, Lanham thought, *but she won't. She'll endure it however long it lasts, and when he's gone she'll weep over his grave. Provided she outlives him.*

Bailey rambled on in anger. "After all I've done for Montoya. Hired him when he needed wages . . . bought land off of him at a price no Mexican would've paid him."

Bet you didn't hurt yourself none, Lanham thought. *You don't give nothing away. When you give, you figure on getting more in return. Even from Zoe.* He reflected a moment. *Especially from Zoe.*

Bailey said, "We'll hang him so high the buzzards'll have to climb."

Blustery talk always got under Lanham's skin. He hated anything false. "You know you can't do that," he put in irritably. "You'd flush them bandits like they was quail. We got to leave Montoya for bait."

Bailey knew it. He was just talking, giving vent to his anger. But he resented being reminded of it by a cowhand. "Neal, I was in this part of the country when you was in short britches."

Lanham couldn't resist an oblique reference to Bailey's age. "I'd forgot about that. You've known Zoe ever since she was a little bitty girl."

Bailey's jaw worked, but no words came. He went back to the subject at hand. "I promise you this: Montoya's as good as dead. When we've sprung the trap and we don't need him anymore, he's dead."

"*When* we've sprung it," Lanham said. "What you do then won't matter."

Zoe said bitterly, "But I want to be there."

*   *   *

The Reyna brothers knelt on either side of Lanham, peering through the pale light of the half moon at the brush shack in which Montoya lived. Lanham had told them he wouldn't order them to make this ride . . . that he would hold no hard feelings if they didn't. But they had elected to come.

On either side of Lanham, half a dozen of Bailey's cowboys squatted in the short grass, watching the dim glow of a candle through an open door and window. More Bailey men, principally his Mexican *vaqueros*, waited in the brush with the horses. They would come running on signal, or at the sound of trouble.

Crouching, Andrew Bailey made his way cautiously to Lanham. "One of my boys thinks he hears horses comin'. You hear anything?"

Time like this, he can afford to recognize me, Lanham thought resentfully. "All I hear is your boots in that dry grass. If you'd get still . . ." He couldn't see the anger in Bailey's eyes, but he could feel it. *Damn good thing he didn't talk Zoe into letting him run her ranch. He'd of fired me before I could've said I quit.*

He heard horses, moving in a slow walk from south of the shack. The riders paused periodically, perhaps listening and looking. Tensing, Lanham brought his saddle gun into position. Gradually he discerned movement deep in murky shadows. A pair of vague forms emerged cautiously from the heavy chaparral. As they approached the shack, a Spanish voice said something sharp and quick in hardly more than a conversational level.

The candlelight went out. A man came out and walked slowly past the corner of the shack. *"Aqui,"* he answered. Two horsemen moved up.

Bailey whispered, "That ain't no dozen men."

Lanham shrugged. "Couple of scouts, comin' in to

make sure everything is *bueno*. The rest are back yonder in that brush."

The low mutter of the men's conversation was barely audible. Their horses stirred restlessly. Suddenly one raised its head and nickered. From behind Lanham and Bailey, from out in the brush where the *vaqueros* waited, came an answering nicker.

It was as if a bomb had gone off at the shack. Montoya shouted. The two riders dropped low in their saddles and wheeled around. Montoya cried out for them to wait for him.

Bailey roared, "Shoot! Don't let a man get away!"

Rifle and pistol fire erupted. Montoya fell gasping. One of the Mexican horses plunged to earth, screaming. Its rider rolled, got up and fell again. The other rider spurred for life.

We spilled it! Lanham angrily pushed to his feet and levered another cartridge into the hot breech of his saddle gun. *Damn it to hell, we spilled it!*

He ran across the yard, pausing once to fire at the fleeing rider. He knew he had thrown the shot away, for he couldn't even see his front sight.

The fallen rider turned over on his side and fired a pistol. Bailey's cowboys and one of the Reynas riddled him. Montoya was bent over on the ground, groaning in pain and gripping a bleeding leg. Lanham saw no sign of a gun around him.

The *vaqueros* brought up the horses. Lanham grabbed his and swung into the saddle. In the moonlight he glimpsed Zoe Daingerfield's excited face. "Damn it, Zoe, I told you to stay back!"

He had as well have tried to tell it to her horse. She spurred after him into the heavy growth of brush.

They ran a mile or so, smelling the dust stirred by the unseen horses ahead of them. Branches slapped his face. Thorns clutched at him, and he felt his shirtsleeves rip from shoulder to cuff. Around him, behind him, he could hear the pounding of hoofs as his pursuing party spurred. He realized it was a lost cause. The way their own group was scattered now, it would be lucky if they didn't start shooting each other in the dim moonlight. He looked around for Bailey but didn't see him.

"Hold it up now, boys," he shouted. "Let's stop right here."

Gradually he saw the men responding to his call and reining in. The riders circled around him. Zoe Daingerfield came up breathing heavily, her blouse rent by some grasping mesquite limb.

"How come we've stopped?" she demanded.

"Because we can't see a damned thing. We could've passed them for all we know. Next thing we'll be potshottin' each other. When my time comes to die, I don't want it to be no accident." He still didn't see Bailey. "Zoe, you sure you're all right?"

She nodded. "I didn't want to give up the chase."

"What chase? They just melted in the dark."

Flames licked above the brush. Somebody had set Montoya's shack afire. In the edge of the crazy, dancing light, Lanham saw Bailey standing, hands on his hips. Bailey said, "Did you get any more of them?"

"Never even seen any," Lanham replied. "What happened to you?"

"Damn fool *vaquero* let my horse get loose before I could grab the reins. Left me afoot. So I finished up things around here, me and Rafael." He jerked his head toward a blocky, dark-faced Mexican who always rode half a pace behind him, wherever Bailey went.

Off to the side of the blazing shack, the dancing firelight played on a pair of sandal-clad feet, suspended far above the ground. Lanham couldn't see the rest of Montoya. He didn't have to.

Zoe took a long look, then turned her face away. "It's

no more than he had comin'." But she looked as though she might turn sick.

In a way, Lanham hoped she would. A woman wasn't supposed to take pleasure in a thing like this; it wasn't true to nature. He put his arm around her shoulder and led her toward her horse. "Come on, Zoe. This is a hell of a sight for you to look at."

She said, "It was my place to be here." He knew she hadn't softened, not yet.

Zoe was a long time saying anything more as they rode back toward Bailey's. Lanham noticed that once or twice she lifted her hand to her shoulder, and for the first time he saw a dark splotch on the torn blouse. Even in the poor light, he knew it was blood. He went cold. "Zoe, did you get hit by a bullet?"

"No, I ran into a limb. I guess I must have a bad thorn."

She reined up. They had dropped behind Bailey and the other riders. Lanham pulled aside a part of the ripped blouse and bent over close. "Still in there. Get down, and I'll take it out before it gets any worse than it already is."

She dismounted and pulled off the blouse. Shaken a little, he took out his pocketknife and probed as gently as he could. She caught her breath short and held it.

Lanham heard horses coming back. The two Reyna brothers rode out of the brush. Zoe quickly held the blouse in front of her. Reynaldo Reyna pretended not to see. "Something wrong, *caporál?*"

"Thorn in her shoulder. Nothin' I can't take care of. We'll catch up directly."

Reynaldo nodded, understanding. "*Sí, caporál.* If the Bailey he asks, we will say you are just behind us."

The thorn was big. With Zoe's shaking hand holding matches, he brought it out with the point of the blade. Then he put his mouth to the soft flesh of her shoulder.

He sucked the wound clean and spat away the salty blood. Zoe trembled, her head against his chest.

"Now, Zoe, it didn't hurt that much."

"Nothin' hurts. Just hold me, Lanham. Hold me tight as you can."

He felt it then in the warmth of her face, the insistent grip of her hands—the same blood excitement that had come over her as a reaction after the run at the Archuletas', the wild, wounded spirit not yet sated on violence. She clung to him fiercely. She spoke no more, but she seemed to be crying out for help. For a fleeting moment she was a helpless girl, floundering, clutching for any straw she could hold to. He felt a tenderness toward her that he had never known and a wish that he could bring her out of this dizzying vertigo of hatred.

The moment passed and the tenderness was gone and she was no longer a girl; she was a woman, a woman who wanted him as desperately as he wanted her, a woman whose turbulence could be quelled only by another form of violence, one that passed for love. Through the fire that took possession of him, one thought intruded, then was quickly lost in the flame:

I was supposed to help her. But how can I help her if I'm lost myself?

After a long time they were close enough to see the shadowy forms of horsemen ahead. Lanham could recognize the Reyna brothers, bringing up the rear.

Zoe broke the silence. "I'm glad I went. I'm glad I saw. I want to be there when we get the next one. I want to be there when we get them all."

"Maybe what happened tonight'll scare them off awhile. There may not be any more."

"There'll be more. Bonifacio told us about Montoya. He'll find out about the others."

Lanham frowned. He wished he knew what to do. He

couldn't beat the hatred out of her, and he couldn't love it out of her.

God help us all, he thought, *if Bonifacio ever makes a mistake.*

Ten

AS THEY UNSADDLED IN ANDREW BAI-
ley's dusty corral, amid tired ponies that pulled away in
relief and rolled sweaty bodies in the sand, Lanham
could sense a dark suspicion in the way the ranchman
peered at him. Lanham took care of Zoe's saddle, then
his own.

Bailey said, "You sure Zoe's all right?"

"Like I told you, just a bad thorn in her shoulder."

"She could've gotten shot. You ought to've stopped
her."

"She don't ask no questions or look back. Zoe wants
to do somethin', she just naturally does it."

He let Bailey make of that what he would. The girl
stood fifty feet away by the corral gate, waiting. Bailey
looked at her, then back to Lanham. Lanham yielded to
a sardonic smile, for he knew Bailey burned with a wish
to know but would not bluntly ask.

And I wouldn't tell you if you did.

Bailey said, "I'll take her up to the house to spend the night with me and the woman." He didn't ask a question; he made a statement. "You'll be all right down here with the rest of the cowboys."

Lanham nodded. "Best part of the night is already over." He watched Bailey stride away stiffly. *He wonders, but he's afraid to find out. He's wished after her for a long time.* Lanham spat. *The hell with him. Let him sweat.*

Bailey would not hear of the idea of letting Zoe go back to her ranch with just Lanham Neal and the two *hombres*. After breakfast he insisted, "I'm sendin' three of my own *vaqueros*." Zoe protested that this would leave him short-handed, but Bailey waved off the objection. "Don't argue. I laid awake thinkin' about it, and I've made up my mind. You need more watching-out-for. These men are dependable . . . as dependable as a Mexican ever gets."

Just how dependable, Lanham found out that night.

He lay on his blanket in his dark *jacal*, smoking a cigarette that tasted like horsehair, his mind running over his many problems—the Slash D cattle, the horses, the *bandidos* . . . and most of all, Zoe. What was he going to do about her? What *could* he do about her? This thing between them, it was getting plumb out of hand. Not in his most shameless dreams when he was working as a cowboy for her father had he ever pictured the situation taking this kind of turn. Sure, he had thought sometimes how fine it would be to marry her, to come home to the warmth of her arms at night, to give love and to receive it in the seemly manner that custom prescribed. But this way was all wrong. A casual dalliance with some saloon girl in a lamplighted back room wasn't considered a mark against a man, for she was *that* kind of woman, and no damage was done. But a man was expected to stand back from a woman of family, a woman of good name, to look at her with his hat in his hand and never

touch her—never even *think* about touching her—until
they had spoken their vows before a preacher and sanc-
tified the relationship in the eyes of God and the state
of Texas.

He hadn't intended it any other way with Zoe; he had
no intention of taking advantage of her. But somehow,
spontaneously, they had slipped into this alliance with
such a surprising ease that he was entrapped before he
realized it. Several times he had told himself the honest
thing would be to leave before they reached the point
of no return. But maybe they already had.

He couldn't just abandon her, the country overrun by
bandits the way it was. If Andrew Bailey were a different
sort, Lanham could take Zoe to his place and leave her
whether she liked it or not. But he had no illusions about
Bailey and what he would do. The thought lay thinly
veiled in the ranchman's eyes every time he looked at
Zoe.

Better me than him, Lanham thought.

He could marry Zoe. He used to think about that
sometimes, when Griffin was alive. But there had always
been a worry that people would think he had done it to
get ahold of this ranch, the way Bailey had married that
Mexican woman. Lanham had too much pride to be
branded a Daingerfield-in-law.

Anyway, what if he asked her and she turned him
down? Times, the way she clung to him, he was sure
she loved him. Other times he had a strong feeling that
what drove her wasn't love but hate, that she was using
him rather than he using her . . . that through him she
found release for built-up bitterness. Times it seemed less
of love than of contest.

For his own part, he couldn't tell for sure if he was
in love with Zoe or if it was just the female magnetism
she had. He had never had much time or opportunity
to be in love with a woman before, even halfway. He

had nothing to compare this experience, no perspective.

Anyway, it was a waste of time trying to analyze the situation. There was no clear way out, no good answer. Wherever introspection ended, he still thought about her . . . still wanted her.

The camp had been quiet an hour or two, and he figured everyone was asleep. He pushed to his feet and started across to Zoe's shack. She would be expecting him. She always did.

A dark figure loomed up out of the shadow. "*Quién es?*"

Lanham could see a rifle. Instinctively he reached for his pistol but found he had left it in the shack. Anyway, he recognized the voice . . . one of Bailey's *vaqueros*.

Irritably he said, "It's me, the *caporál*."

"In the dark it is hard to tell."

"Well, it's me anyway, damn it. What're you doin' here?"

"*El patrón . . . el Señor* Bailey . . . he said for us to watch all the time over the *señorita*. He said it would be our ears if anything happened to her. So nothing happens, *señor. Entiende?*"

"*Entiendo.* But there's nobody here that means her any harm. Now you can go back down to your own end of the yard. I'll do the watchin'-out up here."

"*El patrón*, he said . . ."

"Your *patrón* can run *his* ranch any way he wants to. *I'm* runnin' this one."

The *vaquero* shrugged, resolute. "I work for *Señor* Bailey. I do as he says."

"Stand there, then, till you get moonstroke." Lanham strode back to his own *jacal*. He was coldly certain now that protection from bandits hadn't been Bailey's only consideration in sending these men. Whatever happened here, a full report would get back to Andrew Bailey in short order.

*Well, so be it. I don't see why I give a damn. I don't belong
to him, and neither does she.*

He lay on his blanket alone, but he didn't sleep much.

In the fringe of brush, Lanham stared a long time at the
Galindo place, working up nerve to ride in. He had scru-
pulously avoided this *ranchito* since the night Galindo had
fallen before Vincente's rifle. He ought not to be here
now. He told himself he didn't know why he had come.

But he knew. He was troubled by the memory of that
angry-eyed girl. He realized the notion was probably
crazy, but for a while he had hoped he could settle a
question in his own mind. He had been badgered by a
suspicion that the feelings which Zoe aroused in him
might be stirred by any good-looking girl, that it was
simply man-and-woman and not Zoe herself. He had
thought that if he could look upon Galindo's daughter
and not experience the same wanting, he might be more
confident that what he felt for Zoe was gold coin and
not Confederate paper.

A pair of playing children saw him ride out of the
chaparral and ran shouting to a new *jacal*, built upon
the ashes of the earlier one. Lanham tensed. He didn't
really expect trouble, but he couldn't be sure. Galindo
or one of the women could ram a rifle barrel through
one of the openings that passed for a window and blast
him out of the saddle. In their eyes they had the right.

Señora Galindo hurried to the door and shouted excited Spanish at her scattered children. From the shack
all the way down to the field, he saw them high-tailing
it for the brush to hide. Lanham raised his hand as a
sign of peace, but he doubted the Galindos gave it much
credit. In their situation he wouldn't.

The girl stood in the doorway, a battered old Mexican
escopeta in her hands. If she fired it, the recoil would drive

her against the back wall. She said in Spanish, "That is far enough. We want no trouble."

"I didn't bring any. Put that weapon down before it kills us both."

She held it rigidly. With considerable discomfort, Lanham acknowledged that it was pointed somewhere around his belt buckle. "Don't play around with that trigger."

Cautiously he unbuckled his gunbelt. He drifted his horse to the brush arbor and hung the belt on an ax-cut limb that stuck out. The girl lowered the *escopeta* a little, but she could still blow his foot off.

She said, "You are not welcome here. Who is hiding in the brush?"

"Nobody. I'm here by myself."

"What for?" Her tone was sharp, and now he was close enough to see hostility crackle in her dark eyes. She seemed prettier than he had thought. Anger had a strange undefinable quality that improved a woman's looks, whether it be the flash of her eyes or the dark flush of her cheeks.

He said, "I came to see if your father has recovered."

She glanced down the path toward the field. Turning his head, he saw Galindo coming up toward the *jacal* as if he anticipated a hanging. One arm was still bound. He was thinner; the wound had drawn him down. He stopped twenty feet from Lanham, his face fearful.

"We have done nothing. I swear it."

Lanham shook his head. "No trouble. I wanted to find out if you had done what I suggested . . . if you had moved away."

"We are still here, *señor*."

"I see that. I thought you was smarter."

"The women . . ." Galindo apologized, turning his good hand palm upward. "I said to them, 'It would be wise to do as the Daingerfield *caporál* says.' And they said, 'This is our land; we stay.' What can one do when his women are both stubborn and foolish?"

The girl broke in, "If you have come to run us off, you have wasted your ride."

Lanham frowned. He wondered which she would do if he told her why he had *really* come . . . shoot him or laugh in his face? "I'll give you the same advice I gave you before: get away. But I won't try to force you."

In general, the Mexican male ruled the family. He might receive a certain amount of grumbling from his womenfolk, but with it he usually got obedience. Lanham could tell it wasn't that way with Galindo; his women controlled the household. Galindo trembled in Lanham's presence. *Señora* Galindo looked frightened but determined. The girl showed no fright at all; she showed only that *escopeta* and a pair of dark, resolute eyes.

"I am thirsty," Lanham said. "Could I have water?"

"Is there not water on the vastness of the *rancho* Daingerfield?"

"It is a long way. Anyhow, I am here. A drink of water is not much . . . not nearly so much as what you once offered."

Her cheeks flamed. "Whatever I have promised, I would still give. But I do not think either of us would enjoy it."

"Just the water, that's all I need." He moved closer to her. "I don't even know what your name is, *señorita*."

Defiantly she replied, "You can call me *señorita*."

"Your name would sound better."

"*Adiós* sounds better yet."

Her angry courage reached him, but not in the way Zoe did. Whatever feeling he had toward this girl was more of admiration for spirit than of desire after the flesh. Sure, if he found her thataway inclined, he knew he could accept payment on what she owed him and take pleasure in it. But it wouldn't be with the hungry, helpless compulsion he felt toward Zoe.

He had decided he had found out what he had come for. And he wasn't really thirsty. He touched fingers to the brim of his hat. "Then, *adiós, señorita*."

Eleven

JACINTO REYNA POKED DRY STICKS UN-
der a coffee pot suspended over the fire. His brother
Reynaldo lay sprawled on the bare ground, watching
Lanham Neal pace thoughtfully in the darkness. At
length Reynaldo said, "It is none of my business, *caporál*.
But if it were me I would do one of two things."

Lanham stopped pacing. "What're you talkin'
about?"

"Those men of Bailey's, who stand guard by the *patrona* and her *jacal*. I would dig a tunnel under, or I would
walk over them. I do not like to dig."

"You talk too much."

"A family weakness. But you can trust us, *caporál*, not
to talk when we should be quiet. You cannot trust *them*."
He pointed in the direction of the three Bailey *vaqueros*,
who sat at another fire, playing monte. They hadn't
started their guard duty yet for the night. They wouldn't
until Lanham went to bed.

Lanham sat on his heels and watched the pot, waiting for it to come to a boil. "I didn't trust you two boys at first, not till I had a few days to watch you. One thing I don't understand is why you came here with me and Zoe. It's not the pay."

Reynaldo's face twisted a little. "You needed help, we needed a job. And you were fighting the *Cortinistas*."

"You're Mexican. What you got against the *Cortinistas*?"

Firelight flickered in Reynaldo's face, the shadows dark. "You know only two of us. Once there were three."

The coffee boiled. Jacinto poured in a cup of cold water to settle the grounds. Reynaldo suggested matter-of-factly, *"La patrona*, she might enjoy a cup of this coffee."

Lanham pushed slowly to his feet. "Good idea. I'll go find out."

He carried two cups past the Bailey *vaqueros*. They glanced at each other, no man wanting to arise and start the watch. One stood up to follow, shrugged and settled back to his game, for he was winning.

Sitting in the rawhide-and-mesquite chair, Zoe stared at Lanham in surprise. "First time you've been in this *jacal* in two or three days." Her voice carried a little of resentment.

"Bailey's watchdogs. They been like a grass burr I couldn't shake loose of." He handed her the coffee. "Don't burn yourself."

She frowned. "I thought you'd decided you didn't want to burn *yourself*. You've avoided me, Lanham."

"Bailey didn't send them *vaqueros* over here to protect you from bandits. He sent them to protect you from me."

"I don't need that kind of protection."

"He figures you do."

"Andrew Bailey has his own life. We have ours."

She was too naive to realize Bailey's feelings about her, Lanham decided. She had grown up sheltered out here a long way from town. There was much she didn't know. He said, "You don't want wild stories gettin' out. They can hurt you."

"How? *Outlaws* can hurt me. *Drought* can hurt me. But I don't see why idle stories ought to worry me any."

"Zoe, you got no real idea how the world works." He sipped the coffee, wondering how and if he could explain it. She knew little of what lay beyond the chaparral, of the many differences between the things the world *said* and the things it *did*. Her mother had died before she could teach Zoe the lessons a mother is supposed to pass on to a maturing daughter. Zoe had only a vague idea about the contradictory codes which dictated that natural feelings were wicked and shameful and to be suppressed. If she had been a boy old Griffin Daingerfield would have known better how to explain the markings on the moral pathways. As it was, though, he had only been able to tell her that "this you do, and that you don't do." He hadn't been able to tell her why. That was the reason he had chased off every cowboy who came hopefully looking for a smile from her. Now Griffin was gone.

"Zoe, the time has come for you to find out the way the *gringo* world thinks. People are goin' to force their ways on you whether you want them to or not."

She said stubbornly, "I don't care what people say."

"Not now, maybe, but sometime you will. And then you won't think kindly of me."

"Why? What can anybody do to me?"

"Zoe, you carry the Daingerfield name. It meant a heap to your old daddy, but it won't mean much to anybody else if bad talk puts a stain on it."

Her voice tightened. "You're ashamed of me."

"You know better than that." He touched her hand. "Zoe, I'm tryin' to tell you what other people may think. It'll hurt you someday, more than you have any idea."

"The only thing that hurts me now is when you turn your back on me."

"If I was turnin' my back, I'd of already left."

Her hands moved up his arms and around his shoulders. "I don't know what I'd do if you rode away from me. Don't even *talk* about it."

He knew he wouldn't have the will, even if he made the attempt. He pulled her close. "It's the last thing on my mind."

Reynaldo Reyna called from the darkness. "*Caporál*, a visitor."

Lanham recognized the voice. "*Caporál*, it is me, Bonifacio."

"Come ahead," said Lanham. "We'll light the lantern."

Bonifacio paused in the doorway, nervously turning his sombrero in his big hands. He looked back in worry toward the *vaqueros* of Andrew Bailey. "Are they to be trusted? They know me."

Lanham said, "In your case, they're all right."

Reynaldo brought the coffee pot and an extra cup for Bonifacio, who took it eagerly. His hands trembled so that he spilled much of the coffee. His beard was long and black. In the lantern light, his eyes looked sunken and afraid.

Zoe pressed impatiently. "What's the news? What've you heard?"

Bonifacio looked at the dirt floor. If Lanham had smelled tequila, he would have considered Bonifacio drunk. "I have been everywhere. I have heard much." He paused, until Zoe pressed him to go on. Slowly, unwillingly, he continued, "The Captain McNelly, he has

come with all his *rinches*." That was a word the border
Mexicans used for "Ranger," often as not with a strong
dislike. "He and his men, they have been riding everywhere. They try to keep it a secret, but I know where
they have a camp in the brush not ten miles from here."

Lanham blinked. He had no idea they were so close.
"I don't know that they'll help much," he said, "especially if they operate like the carpetbag State Police. And
why shouldn't they? It's McNelly's old outfit. What can
they do that the other law couldn't?"

Bonifacio shrugged. "They are the *rinches*." He said it
as if the word carried some black witchcraft, some mys-
terious invincibility.

"Sheriff's been tryin' a long time. We still got bandits."

Bonifacio commented, "It is said the sheriff is not
happy. He has no kindness for McNelly, and no help."

Lanham grunted. He was not surprised, for there was
enough ill feeling in this country to go around for everybody, including lawmen. If McNelly were to succeed
where local law had not, it might not bode well for the
sheriff's future, because his office was elective. But, of
course, there was another side to the coin. If McNelly's
tactics proved too strong for the average voter's blood—
even if he succeeded in suppressing the bandits—there
might be a substantial advantage in having opposed him
from the beginning. Lanham remembered old Griffin
Daingerfield remarking once that a man's biggest interests were women, money and politics, and that the older
he got, the smaller his interest in women, the greater his
involvement in politics.

The sheriff was not a young man.

Zoe said, "We made good use of the information you
brought us last time, Bonifacio. We got Montoya."

Hands shaking, Bonifacio reached for the pot. "I
heard."

"You have more news for us now?"

"They plan another raid."

Lanham said, "I hoped they'd think twice about comin' back."

"You killed one of their men, and you killed Montoya. That burns in their blood like yellow mescal. The call is out for tomorrow night." Lanham saw pleasure in Zoe's widening eyes. It was not a cheerful sight. "Tomorrow?" she gasped. "Where?"

"Same country, *mas o menos*." His mouth turned down gravely. "It would be good, *patrona*, if you left this place. Go to Brownsville."

"This is my land, Bonifacio."

"They will have it before they are through. No one can stop them. And if they take you, what they do to you will be terrible."

"If I take them, they won't like it either. And I'll take them. With you for my eyes and ears, and Lanham for my fist, I'll have them all."

Bonifacio's eyes held a sadness Lanham had never seen. "You are *la patrona*. I can only tell you what I think."

"I'm stayin' right here on this ranch."

Bonifacio shrugged, giving up. "Tomorrow, then. That is their plan. I can say no more." He pushed to his feet. "It is better I go now. *Caporál*, you will walk with me?"

"Sure." Lanham followed to where the Mexican's horse stood.

Bonifacio untied the reins and paused, reflecting darkly. "I am a simple man, *caporál*, a *vaquero*. I am not a hero. It is a bad thing, this being a spy."

"I reckon it's not pleasant."

"Some of these people deserve to die, *verdad*, because they are *hombres muy malos*. But there are others. It is bad for a man's soul to help kill another man who thinks he is doing good for his country. I look at their faces and I feel like Judas Iscariot."

"You could just ride away from here and never come back."

Bonifacio looked helpless. "You heard *la patrona*. She said she would put a curse on me."

"She is no *bruja*, no witch. And she's not in league with any."

"Strange things happen along the river."

"Bonifacio, there's no such . . ." He broke off, for he knew he was wasting his breath. The *vaquero* believed.

"The worst of it is that I might have to betray a friend."

"A friend?"

"*Caporál*, you said Vincente de Zavala went to San Antonio. He did not."

Lanham feigned surprise. "What do you mean?"

"I saw him below the river. We came upon each other by accident. He rode by as if he did not know me." Bonifacio's eyes met Lanham's. "It is unthinkable that he would join the *bandidos*. But there he was. What else can we believe?"

Lanham figured the less Bonifacio knew, the better. It was not inconceivable that sooner or later the bandits might put the *vaquero* to a test beyond his endurance. What he did not know, he could not tell. "You're mistaken."

"No, *caporál*, it was not a mistake. So steel yourself. The day may come that you must kill Vincente."

The melancholy Bonifacio disappeared into the darkness of the mesquite. Lanham could sympathize with his guilty feelings about being a spy. Lanham felt the same guilt, sending this hapless, frightened little man back.

Twelve

LANHAM WATCHED BAILEY'S *VAQUEROS*
gesturing as they reported to their *patrón*. Bailey looked
straight at him, and Lanham could smell his hatred the
way he could have smelled bad whisky.

So now he knows for sure. Well, to hell with him.

It amazed Lanham how the Reyna brothers sensed
things. Reynaldo sidled up to Lanham and pretended to
work on his stirrup. "*Caporál*, you had better worry as
much about the Bailey as about the *bandidos*."

"I'll watch him," Lanham said. He *had* for a good
while.

Bailey's ranch was spread out broadly from east to
west, most of the way down to the river. There was no
way of knowing where *Cortinistas* might move into it.
Well before dark, Bailey gathered all the men and struck
out in a long trot, taking the lead. He had made one
half-hearted attempt to persuade Zoe to stay at the house
with his Mexican wife, Josefa, but it did no good. Lan-

ham had known it wouldn't. Bailey's manner with Zoe now lacked some of the careful respect he had always shown her. But Lanham saw no real change in the man's eyes as he looked at Zoe. Bailey still wanted her . . . perhaps even more now that he knew someone else had her.

One by one, Bailey dropped off the men in positions to stand watch. "Now, you all know where I'll be waitin'. Don't any of you get into a mix with them. Don't let them see you. Once you see whichaway they're headed, come to me. We'll hit them all in a bunch, not one at a time."

Bailey didn't look at Lanham as he picked the spot for him to drop off. He hadn't spoken to Lanham all day, or even acknowledged his presence. "Here, Neal," was all he said.

Zoe said, "I'll stay with Lanham."

Resentfully Bailey nodded and rode on without argument. It was dusk before he came back. Ignoring Lanham, he asked Zoe, "Everything all right?"

"It won't be all right till we get those bandits."

"We'll get them. We're fixin' to square a bunch of things." Bailey glanced at Lanham, and Lanham felt a chill.

They watched so long as there was light, and when there was no longer light, they listened. Lanham loosened the cinches and sat on the sparse grass beside Zoe. She touched his hand, then drew back. A poor time to be thinking of love, it seemed to Lanham. Then he decided he had misjudged, for she sat with her head back, listening intently.

The night was quiet except for the occasional chatter of birds quarreling in the mesquite, and now and then the bawl of a longhorned cow whose calf had strayed off. Lanham settled back for a long wait.

It was a longer wait than he expected. Pale streaks

began rising in the east. Sleepy-eyed, Lanham watched daylight reach up over the brush and push back the darkness. He glanced at Zoe stretched out in the grass, her head on her arm, eyes closed, breasts rising and falling with the even tempo of her breathing. She had stayed awake most of the night, but she had finally nodded away a couple of hours ago. She would be angry that he had let her sleep.

Well after daylight, Andrew Bailey reined his fidgeting bay to an abrupt halt, yanking against the bits in a manner he would have fired an employee for. He took a long, hard look at Lanham, then at the sleepy girl just coming awake. "You-all hear anything? Anything atall?"

"Quiet as a Mexican graveyard," Lanham said.

"Maybe you was too occupied to pay attention."

Lanham's fists knotted. "You're tryin' to say somethin', Bailey. I reckon you better not."

Bailey waved him off with an impatient motion of his hand. "Never mind. You sure your information was good, about that raid?"

"Good enough. Maybe they decided to do it *mañana*. That's an old Mexican custom."

After riding on down the line to see after the rest of his men, Bailey came back, his horse foaming at the bit. Bailey was foaming a little, too. "Not a sign, not a damned thing, anywheres down the line. Your man was drinkin' tequila, that's what I think."

Lanham doubted that, but he had no inclination to argue with Bailey. Nothing was likely to alter the man's ideas anyway, so why sweat? Lanham didn't think enough of him to care whether he changed Bailey's mind or not.

Bailey said, "Of course there's always a chance they'll still come, even in the daylight. Mexicans, they don't get in no hurry without there's a posse on their tails. We'll leave some men to keep scoutin' while the rest of us go in and eat. You stay, Neal."

Lanham glanced at Zoe. He didn't figure Bailey would try anything with her so long as he had other men along. "Zoe, you better go."

She didn't argue with him. He figured she was hungry.

Lanham half expected that someone eventually would bring grub to him or relieve him so he could go in. After a few hours he decided he should have known Bailey better than that. He hitched his belt tighter, talked to himself a little and stayed. It wasn't the first time he had gone without when his belly said "eat."

The sun had passed its midday peak when one of the Bailey *vaqueros* loped up excitedly. "*Señor*, I go for the *patrón. Allá . . .*" he pointed west ". . . they are taking horses south, toward the river."

Lanham began tightening his cinch. "Somebody watchin' them?"

"*Sí*, two men. Will you go and help them if there is trouble?"

"I'll go." Lanham felt his spirits rise, and his faith in Bonifacio. "If we have to, we'll hold them at the river till you get back with Bailey and some more guns. *Ándele, amigo.*"

Presently he cut across fresh horse tracks. The way the horses were strung out, he could only guess at the number. Forty or fifty, maybe. Hard to guess how many riders. *I'll find that out soon enough,* he thought soberly, *and I probably won't like it.* He trailed the horses, moving in a long trot. He began to smell fresh dust which hadn't had time to settle.

He spotted the two Bailey riders trailing after the horses at a discreet distance, keeping watch on the men ahead of them. They evidently gave no thought to the possibility of someone coming up behind them. If he had been an outlaw, Lanham could have shot both of them at close range with a pistol before they even knew he was around.

"It's just me," he spoke. "Don't anybody get excited."

They almost fell out of their saddles, trying to shift position to get the drop on him. They recognized him and let their pistols slide back into their holsters. "*Bandidos* just ahead of us, *señor*," one of them spoke quickly. Lanham nodded. The *vaquero* went on, "It was me who saw them first. They were just riding along as if they were on their way to church, driving all those horses."

"How many?"

"About forty horses . . . maybe forty-five."

"I mean how many men? The horses ain't likely to shoot at us."

"Five men, *señor*. It will be easy, when the Bailey gets here. They suspect nothing. They are laughing, singing. They think they will get away with the Bailey his horses."

Lanham shrugged. It made sense, as far as it went. The only thing that bothered him was how the bandits had gotten onto Bailey's country from the river in the first place. They hadn't left any tracks doing it. They could have been playing the game safe, of course. They could have come up somewhat to the west, then cut across to minimize the exposure.

He rode along with the *vaqueros*, well behind the horse herd. *Five men*. Looked like there ought to have been more willing patriots than that to come over here and give the *gringo* Bailey a taste of *Cortinista* revenge. But patriotism was always a variable commodity. Sometimes it talked loudly in a border *cantina* but spoke softly in the gray light of dawn. It was that way on either side of the river.

Bailey finally rode up with the men he had gathered along the way. His face was flushed with excitement.

Lanham noted with displeasure that Zoe was with him. *Damn it, she ought to've stayed at the ranch.* A rifle rested across her lap. *Hell-bent for vengeance. If she don't burn it out of her system, it'll get her killed.*

Stiffly Lanham said, "Well, Bailey, I sure hope you enjoyed your dinner."

Bailey's look was one of hatred. "How many men they got?"

"Five."

"Five?" Bailey sounded disappointed. "We could as easily have taken care of ten."

"We ain't done nothin' about the *five* yet. We just been sittin' here talkin'."

Bailey's face reddened. He motioned with his arm and set his horse into a long trot. The men fanned out on either side of him in a skirmish line. They began over-taking the other riders rapidly.

Lanham suggested, "Just to be safe, Bailey, reckon we ought to be real sure them are your horses?"

"They're on my country. Who else's would they be? If they scare you, Neal, stay back."

It was not so much a battle as a rout, a bloody running fight that lasted perhaps three minutes. For Lanham Neal, it was over in fifteen or twenty seconds.

The men driving the horses were taken by surprise. They never looked back until Bailey fired the first shot. They milled in confusion, abandoning the horse herd and broke into headlong flight.

Lanham never fired. At the distance he figured it would be a wasted shot. Bailey and his *vaqueros* kept shooting anyway. The fleeing horsemen fired back, more in desperation than in hope.

Lanham's horse had just started to jump a low bush when the bullet caught it in the head. Lanham saw the spatter of blood just as the horse's feet left the ground.

He felt the animal jerk and go limp. It is a shattering sensation to have a running horse die beneath you. Lanham had time only to kick his feet free of the stirrups and throw an arm up over his face. There was time, too, for one quick thought: *That shot came from behind me, not from in front.* The ground slammed against him, and the horse's legs struck his shoulder as the animal came over. Lanham lay stunned, mouth half full of dirt, lightning flashing in his eyes. Horsemen rushed by him, and he tensed, waiting for another bullet that didn't come.

That Bailey! That damned Bailey! Wonder how much he paid a vaquero to do it?

He felt Zoe's hands on his shoulders and heard her frightened voice. "Lanham! Lanham!"

That damned Bailey! Bet he's riding off laughing up his sleeve, thinking he's got me killed . . . thinking she's as good as his.

He pushed painfully to his knees, spitting sand, trying to blink the flashing out of his eyes. Zoe attempted to help him to his feet, but he couldn't make it.

"Lanham," she cried, "are you shot?"

He didn't have breath for an answer. All he could do was shake his head and gasp for air. Through burning eyes he could see Bailey and his *vaqueros* fading through the dust, and he could hear the shooting. Lanham rubbed a hand carefully over his shoulder. Pain jabbed like a knife. But he was sure he hadn't been struck by a bullet. When he could speak, he said, "Just the fall jarred me. It was the horse that got shot."

It was hard to tell whether Zoe was more angry or scared. "They might've killed you. I hope Bailey gets every last one of them!"

He could have told her it wasn't horse thieves who had shot his horse. But he decided she wasn't ready to believe anything bad about Bailey . . . not yet.

Zoe looked anxiously after the hard-running horses, and Lanham could tell she was eager to go. He caught her hand. "Stay here, Zoe. You got no business in a thing like that."

"If I don't go now, I can't catch up."

"You don't need to. It's Bailey's ranch, not yours. There's men dyin' up yonder. You got no call to watch."

She gave up, for by now she couldn't have overtaken them anyway. Lanham tried to push to his feet, but he couldn't steady himself. Zoe holding him, he sank back to his knees and stayed there, struggling to regain his breath. He rubbed his shoulder again, wondering if the impact had dislocated it.

Zoe knelt, tears in her eyes. "How bad is it, Lanham?"

"No bones busted, far as I can find. I'll just be sore as hell."

She began wiping dirt from his face with a handkerchief. Done with that, she kissed him sympathetically. "I didn't want you hurt, Lanham. I wouldn't never want you hurt."

He caught her hands with what strength he had. "It hurts me every time I see you come on a ride like this. It ain't noways right, Zoe. You're a woman. I want you to promise me that from now on if there's fightin' to be done, you'll leave it to the men."

"If you didn't love me, Lanham, you wouldn't worry about me. I'm glad for that. But I can't make you a promise. You know why."

"At first I *thought* I knew why. Now I don't think that's reason enough. You're a woman. You ought to act like one."

"I've been a woman with *you*, Lanham. Don't ask me for more than that."

"It'd please me better if you'd just go to Brownsville and get out of this bloody mess."

The shooting was a long way off now and trailing into sporadic firing. The shots finally stopped altogether.

Lanham shuddered, for he knew what that meant. Zoe looked toward the source of the sound, thought the action was out of sight beyond the brush. "They got them, Lanham."

He sensed satisfaction in her voice. "We had them outnumbered. It couldn't have turned out any other way."

"You don't sound pleased over it."

In the back of his mind lingered a strong suspicion that many of the raiders were not so much outlaws as misguided Mexican patriots, defrauded into believing they were doing all this for the glory of Mother Mexico, when the main thing they were doing was putting gold and silver into the ample pockets of red-bearded Juan Cortina. But he didn't say that, for he knew it was not a thought shared by Zoe, and nothing he could say would change the ugly memory of her father lying dead amid the horsetracks left by *Cortinistas* on a cruel foray. He said only, "I'm just glad it's over with."

And I wish it was the last time.

With Zoe's help he finally got to his feet. He staggered over for a look at his horse and saw that it was dead, a fact he had not doubted. He thought about taking his saddle off, but he would need help. He hunted around for his pistol, which he had dropped in his fall.

Zoe said, "They're comin' back."

That made Lanham hunt a little harder, for though he doubted they would do it with Zoe and her own riders present, he couldn't completely dismiss the chance that Bailey or one of his men—probably that evil-eyed Rafael—might try to finish the job they had done on him. He found the half-buried pistol and tried to blow the dirt out of it.

Lanham saw disappointment in Bailey's eyes. "I seen you go down, Neal. Thought sure them bandits had done for you."

Dryly Lanham replied, "Better luck next time."

"Won't be no next time for these," Bailey declared, turning his attention to Zoe. "They've reformed. Permanent."

"All of them?"

"All but one. There was one got away in the brush."

Lanham gritted his teeth, partly in pain and partly in anger. More than one bandit had gone free. One of them was talking to Zoe. But accusing Bailey would be like roping at the moon. What could Lanham prove?

The Reyna brothers struggled to recover Lanham's saddle. The Bailey men rounded up the scattered horses. Lanham limped around gripping his stiffened left shoulder. The way his face burned, he knew he must look like a peeled rabbit. He started examining the animals the *vaqueros* brought in. "Bailey! Them ain't your horses. I don't see a one of them that's got your brand."

Bailey cursed. "You got sand in your eyes." But he began to look for himself, and he showed surprise. A *vaquero* came around the horse herd and said, "*Patrón*, we have saved the horses of the *Señor* Tompkins."

That appeared to be so. Every brand Lanham saw was a T.

Herb Tompkins was a contemporary of old Griffin Daingerfield, a crusty cowman of hardy Texan heritage who never asked for anything and never apologized for anything, either. His main ranch lay north of Bailey's, but Lanham remembered that another part of the T ranch lay south, somewhere down on the river.

Bailey rubbed his hand over his face. Lanham got the impression he was disappointed it wasn't his own horses being stolen. Bailey turned to Zoe Daingerfield. "I been wantin' a long time to get that contrary old reprobate in my debt. He's too damned independent to suit me."

"Right now," said Zoe, "I'm a lot more worried about

Lanham. He took a bad fall. We need to get him back to your place to rest."

Bailey made no show of sympathy. "Never seen the cowboy yet that you could kill with a hickory club. But I reckon one of them T horses is good enough for him. Rafael, rope out that Roman-nosed gray for Neal."

Bailey knew horses; Lanham would grant him that. He had glanced into the *remuda* and picked out the meanest-looking animal in it.

Reynaldo Reyna saddled him for Lanham and asked quietly, "You want me to try him first? You look in no condition to ride broncs."

Lanham gritted, "I'll ride *this* one if it kills me." It almost did. The gray pitched a few jumps. Any other time, Lanham could have ridden him without missing a puff on his cigarette. The horse jolted him hard, but Lanham stayed. Afterward, they started for Bailey's.

He lay on the hard plank floor of the front gallery most of the afternoon. Periodically Zoe applied a cool, wet cloth to his skinned face. It helped his feelings, if nothing else.

Late in the afternoon he heard horses and sat up. Bailey walked out onto the gallery, squinting against the sun. A bearded old brush-country cowman rode up, flanked by half a dozen grim *vaqueros*. This was Tompkins.

"Bailey," Tompkins called, "I got trouble. Raiders. They killed some of my men and took a lot of my horses."

Bailey stepped confidently down from the gallery to meet him. "You must've missed the man I sent to tell you. We got your horses back. I got them penned yonder in my big corral."

The old cowman's bearded jaw dropped in surprise. For a moment a grin broke over his face. Suddenly it was gone, and the gray color of his beard seemed to spread over his cheeks. "How'd you get them?"

"We jumped the raiders over west of here. We killed four of them. One got away."

Something in the old man's face brought Lanham to his feet. Instinct told him something was badly wrong.

Tompkins' voice was cold as cemetery clay. He pointed to one of his riders. "Here's the one that got away. He's one of my own. This mornin' I sent five men south with horses, bound for my river ranch." His stubby finger jabbed straight at Bailey. "You miserable, stupid, bloodlovin' son of . . . You killed four of my Mexican cowboys!"

Thirteen

IT HAD BEEN A LONG, SAD RIDE HOME.
Zoe sat weeping in her *jacal*. Lanham paced the yard in
the dusk, the shoulder hurting him every step. The
Reyna brothers hunched beside their fire, sipping black
coffee in silence. None of the Bailey *vaqueros* had returned with them.

In his mind Lanham kept hearing the faraway sound
of the Tompkins riders, singing as they drove the horses.
It was a Mexican song he had known for years, one he
would never forget if he lived to be a hundred. He
walked to the fire and tried some of the coffee out of the
Reynas' pot. Usually they made fair coffee, but tonight
it wasn't fit to drink. Or maybe Lanham just wasn't fit
to drink it. He sipped a little and turned the cup upside
down. Reynaldo glanced at him, then looked away,
nursing his own sorrow. The Reynas had been in on the
chase all the way. Lanham didn't dare ask them if they
had shot anybody.

He looked toward Zoe's shack. She hadn't been out since they had reached home. "I'll go try and talk to her again." He spoke more to himself than to the Reynas. "Not that it'll do any good."

He found her sitting in the rawhide chair, staring at the dirt floor. He lighted the lamp, and he could see the redness of her eyes. "Come on out, Zoe, and get you some air. You ought to eat you some supper, too."

She shook her head, not answering.

"Wasn't your mistake; it was Bailey's."

"It was everybody's mistake. We were all in on it."

"Well, it's done." He couldn't dismiss it the way Bailey had tried to, telling everybody within earshot that it didn't matter much anyway, that they were just Mexicans. It was a wonder to Lanham that Bailey managed to keep any Mexican *vaqueros*, much less his wife. "Zoe, nothin' you or anybody can do will change what's already happened. Main thing is to be sure nothin' like it ever happens again."

"How can we be sure of that?"

"For one thing, if any more shootin's to be done, we'll leave it to McNelly and his Rangers. That's what they come for."

Zoe's tears still trailed down her cheeks. "Why didn't those bandits come, Lanham? If they'd come like they was supposed to, this wouldn't have happened."

"We can't blame this on the bandits. We done it ourselves."

"At least you have one consolation, Lanham. You didn't kill anybody."

"I might have, though, if one of Bailey's *vaqueros* hadn't shot the horse out from under me."

"One of Bailey's . . . What do you mean?"

He hadn't meant to say it. The words had slipped out. Now he'd have to go on with it. "Wasn't the Tompkins cowboys who killed my horse. That bullet came from behind me."

"You sure?"

"Sure's I'm standin' here."

She puzzled. "Must've been an accident."

"You bet it was. He figured on killin' me."

Zoe stared, not believing. "Not Bailey. Why would he?"

"Next time you're around him, Zoe, watch the way he looks at you. He wants you bad enough to kill who-ever stands in his way. And I'm standin' in his way."

"Lanham, you're wrong."

He shrugged. "You just watch him, that's all."

At least she wasn't crying anymore. He had gotten her mind off of that, for the moment. She held her si-lence a long time. Finally she took his hand. "Lanham, what'll we do?"

"We'll stop worryin' about killin' bandits, that's one thing. If Bonifacio brings any more reports, we'll send him to the Rangers. We'll be busy enough just takin' care of this ranch."

"The men who killed my father . . . they're still down there somewhere."

"They'll get caught up with, sooner or later. A man pulls a knife often enough, somebody'll eventually cut his throat for him. Let God take care of them, Zoe."

She shook her head. "His vengeance goes awful slow, sometimes."

"But He gets the last crack at them. Some day they all got to stand there in front of that gate and let Him pass judgment. So *let* Him pass judgment. We got a ranch to run."

She didn't reply.

Into that brooding camp, Bonifacio came back. Lanham could tell by the set of the *vaquero*'s shoulders that he hadn't heard. Bonifacio looked almost cheerful in comparison to his last visit here. He swung down from the saddle and walked straight to the Reynas' fire. "How about some coffee?" When the Reynas just sat and looked at him blankly, he said again, "It's been a long ride, and I'm dry. How about some coffee? What's the matter with you *hombres* . . . you *borracho* or something?"

Lanham strode out with his hands shoved deep into his pockets. "No, Bonifacio, they're not drunk. Get you a cup."

Bonifacio looked at him in the firelight, puzzling. He poured the coffee. "Thought I should come and tell you, *caporál* . . ."

"Tell me what?"

"Tell you the *bandidos* didn't cross the river after all."

"We found that out."

"Is that why you all look so *triste*? You didn't kill any bandits."

"No, no bandits."

"It is just as well. You don't have to carry any of them on your conscience. And neither do I."

Lanham couldn't return Bonifacio's gaze as the Mexican squatted on his heels by the fire. He looked into the glowing coals, flexing his hands. "How come they didn't ride across?"

"A strange thing, *caporál*, a thing to make your blood run cold. They had it planned to come, and then the thing happened. Three of the men who would lead it, they died."

"Died?"

"All the same night, but not together. Each one in a different place, but each the same way, his throat slit from one ear across to the other. It would have been a horrible sight, except . . ."

"Except?"

"Except every one of them had been on the raid here,

the one that killed the *patrón* Daingerfield. A thing to make a man wonder, no?" Bonifacio shuddered. "It is as if the *patrón* his angry spirit had come to take revenge. Perhaps he is here with us now, in this dark."

A chill ran down Lanham's back. He knew what vengeful spirit had been on the prowl. Vincente de Zavala! The irony of it cut him deep. Vincente had killed three of the guilty. But because of that, four innocents had died.

Bonifacio said, "They are saying it is the evil eye. Another bandit was hit by the *susto*, the great fright. A *curandero* broke an egg under his bed and passed the shell over him, and the egg went cloudy. It is a sure mark of the evil eye. Do you think it could be the *patrón* himself?"

Lanham didn't try to answer the question. "We made a mistake today, Bonifacio. We was out huntin' those bandits you said was comin'. We killed four men. Turned out they wasn't bandits. But they're dead, just the same."

The cup sagged in Bonifacio's hands, and most of the coffee spilled on his boots. He did not notice it. He stared at Lanham, and slowly he seemed to draw into an agonized knot. "Four men?"

"Four men."

Bonifacio slowly turned his hands, looking at them. "It is there, then, the blood. I can feel it, cold as death."

"You're not responsible. The rest of us, but not you."

"Who was killed?"

"*Vaqueros* from the Tompkins ranch."

Bonifacio slumped, his sorrow beyond measuring. "I had friends there."

"You didn't shoot anybody."

"Judas Iscariot did not nail Jesus to the cross."

Zoe came out of her *jacal*. "Did I hear Bonifacio?"

The Mexican didn't answer. Lanham replied, "Yes, Zoe. I just told him."

She came to the fire and saw the Mexican's distress. "Don't accuse yourself, Bonifacio. It was those bandits' fault. They'll pay for it."

Lanham looked up, half inclined to argue the point. But what was to be gained?

Zoe asked Bonifacio why the bandits hadn't come, and he told her. She nodded grimly at Lanham. "Vincente."

Lanham wished she hadn't said it, but he replied, "I reckon."

Bonifacio didn't comprehend. "What is this about Vincente?"

Lanham frowned. The subject shouldn't have come up, but there it was. "I lied to you about Vincente. He didn't go north; he went south. He went for blood."

Zoe said with satisfaction, "And he got it."

Bonifacio blinked. Things were starting to add up for him. But he had one puzzle. "Tonight I rode by the Galindo place. I found him crippling around, and he told me Vincente had shot him. Why would Vincente shoot Galindo if he was only after outlaws? You didn't tell me about that, *caporál*."

Zoe's eyes sharpened. "You didn't tell *me*, either."

Defensively Lanham said, "Vincente made a mistake, that's all. You had any supper, Bonifacio? We'll fix you somethin'."

"I ate at Galindo's." Bonifacio was not about to be sidetracked. "Vincente is not one to shoot a man without reason."

Zoe began pressing, too. "He's right, Lanham. Vincente wouldn't shoot a man unless he had cause for it. And you wouldn't lie to me without cause. Now, how come you did?"

"I didn't lie to you."

"You didn't tell me the whole story. That's the same thing." Anger was rising in her voice.

Trapped, Lanham ground his teeth together. Well, hell, it all had to come out sometime. "The day it all happened, nobody was in a mood to reason. It was a plain-out mistake, and I figured the less said the better. But all right: when Vincente found his wife and old Griffin dead, he started lookin' for somebody to kill. He took a notion Galindo had throwed in with the bandits, so he put a bullet in him. That's all; he just jumped off the deep end."

"He must've thought he had a good reason."

"We found a wounded bandit hidin' in the brush close to Galindo's. I told you about him. He's the one Vincente killed."

"You told us about the bandit; you didn't tell us about Galindo."

Lanham was sweating. "I didn't see any real evidence against him. And I figured if I said anything, somebody'd ride over there and shoot him like a dog."

Zoe's voice was sharp. "Like a *mad* dog!" She turned on him. "You had no right to keep this from me, Lanham . . . no right."

"If you could see yourself now, you'd know why I done it. You got killin' in your eyes, Zoe."

"And why not? That Galindo, he's fed his family off of Daingerfield beef for years. My daddy could have hung him a dozen times, and *should* have. Vincente knew, if *you* didn't. The only thing I can't understand is why he didn't finish the job and kill him."

"I stopped him, that's why. I figured he was wrong."

Her eyes were narrowed. "I think I'd rather trust Vincente's judgment in this than yours. He knows these people, he's one of them."

"You don't shoot a man on suspicion."

"Don't you?" In the flicker of firelight, the deep shadows made her face look a little like old Griffin Daingerfield's. And she sounded like him. "I'll decide that for myself. We're ridin' over there, Lanham."

Reluctantly he said, "I'll take you in the mornin'."

"Not in the mornin'. Now!"

"This time of the night? Don't talk like a crazy woman. It's waited all these weeks. It'll wait till mornin'."

"I'm goin' tonight, Lanham, with you or without you. And if I decide Galindo has had a hand in this, I'll kill him."

She wasn't bluffing, he realized with a chill. She was old Griffin's daughter. "That's why you're not goin', Zoe. You're goin' to go back to your *jacal* and get yourself some sleep, and then we'll thrash this thing out tomorrow. You'll see things clearer in the daylight."

"I'll see to shoot that Galindo. I can do that in the dark." She turned. "Reynaldo, catch me a horse. Catch one for you and your brother, too. I'll want you-all to go with me."

Reynaldo looked at Lanham. Lanham shook his head. "No, Reynaldo. Just stay right where you're at."

She turned on Lanham in fury. "*I* own this place, not you. *I'll* give the orders."

"Not this order."

"You're fired, Lanham Neal. Get off of my place."

"I'm stayin' right here. Somebody's got to keep you from makin' a mistake, Zoe. I'm stayin', and so are you."

She turned sharply and moved toward the *jacal*. She stopped then, looking angrily back over her shoulder. "If you won't help me, I'll bet Andrew Bailey will."

Before anyone could stop her, she trotted to Bonifacio's tied horse, shoved a foot into the stirrup and swung up, her skirts flaring out and riding high up her legs. She shouted at the horse and broke him into a run. Lanham lunged at the reins but missed. The horse struck him with its shoulder and sent him stumbling. The pain of today's fall pounded through him again. On hands and knees, breathing the dust left by the horse's hoofs, he stared in dismay at the darkness which had swallowed her up.

Reynaldo came running. "Maybe we can catch her, *caporál.*"

Lanham pushed to his feet. Futility had a taste like lye soap. "Time we got our horses caught and saddled, she'd be too far off in that dark. We never would find her." He gripped his shoulder, for the pain was considerable. "Bonifacio, you said you know where the Rangers are camped at. Reckon you could find the place tonight?"

"I could get close. With daylight, I could find it in a hurry."

"That's what you better do, then. Go fetch that carpetbagger and as many Rangers as he can spare. Get them over to Galindo's as quick as you can. It may take them all to stop a shootin'." He turned to Reynaldo and Jacinto Reyna. "I'm goin' to go see what I can do to get Galindo the hell out of the way."

"We'll go with you," said Reynaldo.

"It'll mean your jobs."

The brothers looked at each other and made their decision in a hurry. "Today we helped kill four men," Reynaldo replied. "Perhaps the saints will like us better if now we help you save one."

"Thanks, *amigos.* We better be gettin' after it."

Fourteen

GALINDO WAS NOT SO CRIPPLED AS LAN-
ham had thought. Fear grabbed the *ranchero*, and he took
little time rolling up a blanket with a few supplies in it,
catching a horse and striking out for the river in a lope.
He left his family behind with no more than a hasty
adiós.

If they caught him, they wouldn't have much, Lanham
thought disgustedly, looking off into the early-morning
darkness, listening to the fading hoofbeats. He turned to
Señora Galindo, somehow apologetic even though he
knew he had no reason to be. If Galindo had no more
pride than to abandon his family, it wasn't any fault of
Lanham's. "I see you have an oxcart," he said in Spanish. "Pick out what you want to take, and we'll load it
for you. We'll have you on your way by daylight."

"On our way to where?" The chunky Mexican
woman frowned. "We have nowhere to go. This is
home."

"Not for long. They won't let you live here anymore."

"Our name is on the papers in the house of the law in Brownsville."

"It's a long way to Brownsville. Besides, they have your husband's name on *another* list. We'd better get you started."

Señora Galindo just stood there. The daughter spoke sternly, "My mother is trying to tell you, we are not going. Here we are; and here we stay. With Papa or without him."

Lanham turned to the Reynas. Reynaldo made a gesture which said in essence that if a foolish woman has made up her mind, there is little use in a man making a fool of himself also by arguing with her.

"When those people get here," Lanham warned, "their inclination will be to burn this place down around your ears, the way Vincente did."

The girl said, "You can stop them."

He did not share her confidence. "Even if we managed to talk them out of it—which I doubt—your father is gone. You'd have to work this place without his help."

Her eyes said what her lips could not, for it would be disrespectful: *we always did.*

Lanham tried to think of other arguments, but nothing came to mind that he thought would sway these women. He shrugged, finally. So be it. All he could do now was wait. "You have any coffee? I'd sure like to fix some."

He built a fire in the outdoor pit and boiled coffee in a bucket. It didn't taste very good, but it gave him strength, and it gave him something to do with his hands while he waited for daylight. He wondered where Bonifacio was, and if he really knew how to find the Ranger camp or if he had just been bragging.

The children had stirred out of their sleep briefly when their father left, but they had returned to their blankets. The mother and the oldest daughter didn't go back to bed. They sat in front of the house near Lanham and the Reynas, waiting in passive silence. Lanham looked at first one of them, then the other. He spent a lot more time studying the girl than her mother. It seemed to him she could be a surpassingly pretty girl in her own way if she had some American-woman clothes and fixed herself up American-woman style. But he knew that was just prejudice; he ought to accept her by her own standards. To the Mexican people she probably looked fine just the way she was. The longer Lanham stared at her, the better she looked to him. He decided it was unfair to judge her by any measure other than her own. She was young; that was the main thing. To him, most young girls looked pretty unless they ate too much and got fat. There probably had never been enough food around here anyway. She had pleasant features. Beyond that she had a spirit that must have come from her mother's side of the family, for Galindo hadn't shown any.

Good thing for Galindo he's got strong women, or he wouldn't even own a pair of britches, Lanham thought.

The cup gradually went cold in his hands. He nodded off to sleep. After a while Reynaldo Reyna awakened him with a gentle nudge. Lanham looked up startled, into the sunrise.

"Horses, *caporál.*"

Lanham heard them. He pushed to his feet. "Sure do hope it's those Rangers." But he had a strong feeling he wouldn't be that lucky. He got his rifle and motioned for the Reyna brothers to split up, one on each side of him. He motioned for the women to go into the *jacal.*

Andrew Bailey and Zoe Daingerfield broke out of the brush, followed by half a dozen of Bailey's riders. Lanham raised his rifle to the ready but avoided pointing it at anyone. The Reynas were not so particular. They pointed theirs at a couple of the Bailey men who had spent so much time at the Daingerfield place, watching Zoe and Lanham.

Bailey and Zoe came up close and stopped. Zoe's eyes were angry. "We came for Galindo."

"Too late. He's already *por allá*, across the river."

"I saw the women run for the shack. He wouldn't go off and leave his family."

"The hell he wouldn't."

Zoe looked at him hard, until she evidently made up her mind he wasn't lying. "All right then, he's gone. But we'll make sure he don't have anything to come back to." She pointed at the remains of the fire where the coffee bucket sat. "Let's burn it, Andrew."

Lanham said, "Let's not."

Zoe blinked. Bailey said, "You won't stop us, cowboy." He swung down from the saddle and took a step toward the fire. He stopped abruptly, looking down the muzzle of Lanham's rifle.

"I'll stop *you*," Lanham told him.

Bailey's mouth dropped open. "You won't kill me."

"Why not? You tried to kill *me*. Difference is, I'm a heap sight closer to the target."

Lanham allowed himself a cautious glance at the *vaqueros* and saw that the Reynas had them under control. The only one Lanham had to worry about was Bailey. And, perhaps, Zoe.

In a minute he knew he didn't have to worry about Bailey, not unless he turned his back on him. Bailey tried to show defiance, but fear seeped into his eyes. *I got him,* Lanham thought. *Get the drop on him and he's like a dog— all bark and no teeth.* "Climb back up on that horse, Bailey."

Bailey tried to stare him down, but Lanham thrust the rifle barrel forward. Bailey backed off, putting his left hand up on his horse's mane, the right on the saddle-horn.

Zoe's voice was bitter. "How come you're doin' this, Lanham?"

"Because what you're fixin' to do is wrong. Shootin' people, burnin' them out . . . that ain't your true nature, Zoe. One of these days this sickness is goin' to leave you, and you'll hate what you've done. We can't undo what we did yesterday, but we can stop before we do any more. Let me take you home."

Anger mottled her face. "When I finish what I came to do, I'll go home. You won't be goin' with me."

She wasn't through yet; he could tell that. *Where the hell is Bonifacio at with them Rangers? What if he got lost in the dark? What if they moved their camp?*

Lanham made up his mind to stall her as long as he could. Maybe if he kept her talking, the anger would boil out of her and she'd start thinking on a straight line again. Maybe she would get out of the notion, though offhand he couldn't remember any notion he'd ever seen her get out of if she had once made up her mind about it.

Zoe hadn't come here to argue. She swung her leg over the man's saddle she was riding and dropped to the ground, skirts flaring. Resolutely she moved toward Lan-ham. He backed away, trying to maintain the distance between them. She leaned over and took a burning stick out of the fire.

"Call them women and tell them to get out of that shack. I'm fixin' to touch it off."

"There's kids in there, Zoe. You burn that *jacal*, they got no place to live."

"Tell them, Lanham."

"No, Zoe. You're not going to burn that shack."

He heard a commotion behind him but didn't dare

look back. He could tell that the women and the children were coming out, scared.

Zoe watched them. Most of all she watched the girl. "Now maybe I see why you were so interested in protectin' these people, Lanham. I didn't know they had a girl like that."

"I never touched, her, Zoe. Never intended to."

She didn't believe him. She started toward the shack, holding the blazing brand in front of her. Lanham said, "Stop, Zoe."

She kept moving, her eyes on him. He raised the rifle to his shoulder. She paused in doubt, regained her confidence and started again. Lanham aimed the rifle. When she didn't stop, he took a half breath and squeezed the trigger. The brand leaped from her hand, showering her with sparks and splinters. With a startled cry she jumped backward, her eyes hurt and bewildered. Bailey reached for his pistol but caught himself and raised his hands again as the muzzle of Lanham's rifle jerked toward him, smoking.

The surprise drained from Zoe's eyes, and her jaw set hard. "That proved it, Lanham. You won't shoot me." Leaning down, she picked up the bullet-shattered stick. A blaze still clung stubbornly to it. She started toward the shack again. Lanham backed slowly, keeping in front of her.

"Zoe . . ."

She kept walking.

When she was two paces from the shack, he knew there was only one way to stop her. He brought the rifle to his shoulder again. "Zoe, stop!"

Glaring, she took another step. Cold sweat broke across his face. "God help me," he whispered, and he fired.

She screamed. The stick dropped to her feet. She staggered backward, clutching at her arm.

Bailey stood like stone, gray with fear. The *vaqueros* froze in their saddles. Zoe slowly went to one knee. Blood ran between her fingers. Her face was white as milk.

Lanham dropped the rifle and ran to her. He grabbed her to keep her from sagging to the ground. "Zoe, I didn't want to do it."

Tears ran down Zoe's cheeks. She turned her head to look at the wound. Lanham ripped the sleeve away and saw his aim had been good. The bullet had not bitten deeply enough to strike bone. "I'm sorry, Zoe. You made me do it."

Zoe jerked away from him, her eyes bitter. The Galindo women took over. They stanched the flow of blood. *Señora* Galindo brought fresh goat's milk and cleansed the wound while Zoe sat in resentful silence, wincing. She wouldn't look at Lanham, but she stared at the girl, hating her.

One shot had taken the fight out of Bailey and his men.

"Zoe," Lanham said, "you're goin' to get a whole lot sicker before you get any better. Send Bailey and his bunch on back. I'll take you home when you're able to go."

Her gaze swung slowly to him, her eyes clouded. "You won't take me anywhere, Lanham Neal. If ever you set foot on my place again, you'll be shot. If I can do it, I'll shoot you myself." She looked around for Bailey. "Andrew, take me home."

Bailey stepped forward, arms outstretched to take her. He helped her onto her horse, then swung into his own saddle. He paused for a last word. "Takes a lot of guts, Neal, to shoot a woman."

Lanham made no reply. *It took more than anybody will ever know,* he thought, suddenly shivering. He stood and watched until they disappeared into the brush, and he listened until they faded beyond hearing. He turned finally to the Reynas. "We're out of a job . . . all of us."

Reynaldo shrugged. Jacinto said, "We have been out of a job before."

"I didn't want to shoot her. I hope you know that."

"We know. If you had to do it again, you would have to do the same."

Lanham looked down at the stick of wood Zoe had dropped. Some of her blood still spotted the ground. "I don't know. I doubt I could."

The Galindo girl brought a basket-covered jug from the shack and held it out to Lanham. "You need this."

He took out the corncob stopper and tipped the jug three times before he passed it on to the Reynas. The girl stared at him a long while, her eyes grateful. She said, "Words aren't enough."

The tequila churned in him. "Words'll do. I didn't ask you for anything; I don't expect anything."

She was a desirable girl, but he didn't want to think about that. He wanted to think about Zoe. "Better go see after your mother. I think this whole thing has left her a little sick."

Reynaldo watched the girl go. Philosophically he said, "It is not all bad, *caporál*. You have lost one woman, but you have gained another."

The Rangers came, finally. Lanham muttered under his breath and pushed to his feet, waiting while they rode across the clearing. He looked a moment at Bonifacio, silently cursing him for being so slow. Then his gaze went to the slight, bearded man who led the riders. This must be McNelly. Lanham was not much impressed by the looks of him. From the stories he had heard, McNelly should have stood seven feet tall.

Bonifacio spurred out in front, relief washing across his face as he saw that the place was still intact. "I was afraid, *caporál*. But I see we got here in time."

"In time, hell; you're too late."

"I see no damage done."

Lanham pointed to the blood on the ground. "It was done. *La patrona* was shot."

Bonifacio slumped, till Lanham told him the wound was not serious. "Go to her, Bonifacio. She'll need help. You're the only old hand she has left."

Lanham went back to the coffee bucket. By now the coffee had boiled black and vile, but it went with the way he felt.

McNelly came to him presently. "Mind if I have a cup of this?" There was a pallor to his skin. He looked as if he needed something more medicinal than coffee. Lanham said, "Help yourself. You'll regret it."

"Those *vaqueros* of yours, they told me what happened. Today and yesterday. I can imagine how you feel."

"Can you?"

"As I understand it, this Galindo is a thief, possibly even in league with the river bandits."

"Could be. We don't know that for a fact."

"This Galindo girl . . . something between you and her?"

Lanham cut the captain a sharp, angry glance. "You ask a hell of a lot of questions. No, I never even seen her but once or twice in my life. Never was within three foot of her."

"That's what I figured. So what you did today, you did because you knew it was right, and not for personal reasons."

"I had a personal reason. I had to stop Zoe before she . . . before *we* . . . went any farther than we already had. I stopped her because she was wrong." He clenched his teeth. "Always did seem like I brought hard luck to everybody I was ever around. I sure didn't do *her* no good."

"She means a great deal to you, doesn't she?"

"Like I said, you ask too damn many questions."

"I've had to do things I didn't like, Neal, things I regretted and *will* regret to the last day I live. But they were duty. Duty comes first, if a man thinks anything of himself."

"I wasn't thinkin' about duty. Last time I worried about duty, some damn Yankee shot me in the hip."

"Maybe you didn't figure it as duty, but that's what was beneath it." McNelly's face twisted at the taste of the coffee, and he spat it out. A show of judgment, Lanham thought.

McNelly said, "I take it you're out of a job."

"I'm a fair-to-middlin' cowboy. I'll find work."

"Some of my recruits quit when they found out how things really are down here. Maybe I could use you."

"I bring bad luck to everything I touch."

"That's a foolish notion."

Lanham's face creased. He saw no reason he ought to like this man. "Folks say you're a carpetbagger."

McNelly shrugged. "I've heard that."

"I was a Confederate soldier."

"So was I." McNelly studied Lanham with a keen, steady gaze. "By what you did today, I take it you feel that this border trouble has gone far enough. I came here to put a stop to it. I can use your help, but I won't beg you. I won't even ask you again. You can take it or leave it."

Feisty little booger, Lanham thought, if he was a carpetbagger. Lanham sipped the coffee, his eyes shut. Damn, this stuff *had* gone to the bad. A man who'd drink this would do anything. He finished the cup.

He didn't ask about the pay. He didn't ask what his job would be. He asked only, "When do we start?"

Fifteen

BEING IN MCNELLY'S RANGERS RE-
minded Lanham somewhat of service in the Confederate
army, and that was not particularly a recommendation.
Captain ran it like a military organization. They rode in
columns, and they moved on strict command. The
thought of Ranger service had never entered Lanham's
mind, so he had nourished no preconceived notions. If
he had, he wouldn't have pictured it like this.

McNelly had no place for the Reynas, so they bade
Lanham *adiós* and went on the drift. It didn't seem to
bother them. As native Mexicans they eyed the Anglo
rinches with a certain natural doubt and wouldn't have
joined the outfit if they had been asked. Though being
out of something to do had always bothered Lanham,
he had observed that the Mexican people didn't fret over
it much. They accepted it passively, the same way they
took other ill fortune. They went hungry sometimes, but
they had faith they would never starve to death.

Captain had spoken with Lanham perhaps five minutes at the Galindo place. Once he enlisted him, he didn't talk to him again. He assigned him to a "dab" and turned his back. From then on, it was as if McNelly had never met him. The captain rode at the head of the column, brooding and withdrawn. Even with a company of Rangers behind him, he seemed somehow a man alone.

What the Rangers called a "dab" was more or less what Lanham remembered from army days as a squad, groups of about eight men each, if each dab was up to strength. Not all of them were. In charge of Lanham's dab was a tall, bestubbled sergeant who wore a Mexican-style sombrero and heavy Mexican spurs. And old border man, Lanham judged him. At least he had probably seen service down this way before. *"Ben acá"*, the sergeant beckoned to Lanham when they reached camp. The words were an Anglo corruption of a colloquial Mexican summons. Lanham followed him to the headquarters tent. There the sergeant dug out a duty book, made an entry and had Lanham sign it.

"I want the terms understood right now, so there won't be no questions asked later or no misunderstandin' with Captain," the sergeant said. "The pay is thirty-three dollars a month in state scrip. Maybe you can get it cashed and maybe you can't. The state'll feed you, when you get fed atall. You furnish your own horse. If he gets killed in line of duty, the state'll pay for him . . . in scrip. You furnish your own pistol; the state'll furnish shells. It don't want them wasted. When you shoot at somethin', hit it." He paused, waiting to see how it was soaking in on Lanham. "We come into some luck in Corpus. Storekeeper set us up to a bunch of Sharps rifles. Here's yours."

He handed Lanham one. Lanham thought it probably was the heaviest weapon he'd ever hefted. He broke it open and looked. Fifty caliber. Buffalo gun, was what it was.

"This thing," he said, "would blow a man half in two if you was to hit him with it."

"If you shoot at a man, you *better* hit him," the sergeant warned. "Captain don't want nobody in his outfit who goes around missin'."

Lanham frowned, running his hand over the piece. It wasn't something a man would carry lightly, or use without doing some tall thinking about it.

The sergeant handed him five cartridges. They weighed like a pouchful of rocks. "If them won't fit your cartridge belt, carry them in your pocket. When you've shot five bandits, you'll get five more cartridges."

Lanham nodded. "When do we ride again?"

"When Captain tells us to."

"He's bound to have a plan laid out."

"Captain's always got a plan, but nobody asks questions; they just do like he tells them, *when* he tells them."

"You mean all these men go along blind, like the tail on a dog, lettin' him send them into God knows what?"

"He don't send you, he *leads* you. You want to scratch your name off the roster and give back that rifle?"

Lanham looked toward the cook's wagon. "I come this far; I'll stay awhile. Besides, looks like pretty soon it'll be time to eat."

Red beans, hardtack and a little sidemeat made up the menu. There were extra plates in the wagon but no cups, and Lanham didn't have one of his own, so he had to pass up the coffee. A couple of young Rangers came over and squatted beside him, setting their plates down. One extended his hand. "Name's Joe Benson." He didn't look as if he had ever shaved and still didn't really need to. "This here is Cebe Smith." Lanham shook hands with both of them. Benson said, "You can drink out of my cup with me till you find you somethin'. How's the dinner?"

Lanham answered with a shrug, for if he answered that he liked it, he would be lying, and that was no example to set for the young. Smith said, "It ain't always like this. Sometimes we ain't got sidemeat."

Benson laughed, "Don't let him scare you. Most of the time we got beef. Usually always some rancher gives us a critter to butcher. But when we run short and there's no rancher, we're out of luck. Captain won't let us kill a beef without it's given to us or we buy it."

He held out his coffee cup, handle forward. Lanham took it gratefully. Eating, he let his gaze run over the Rangers. They were a varied lot, most of them younger than himself. A few he judged probably were war veterans, but most had been too young to serve. *Boys*, was his first thought. *What the hell they doing here? They ought to be home helping their daddies chop cotton.* But a closer study told him they looked able enough for it. Young or not, they all had one thing in common: a determined, self-confident look in their eyes. Dusty and worn, perhaps, but every one of them appeared fit enough to saddle up and make thirty miles before dark.

Joe Benson and Cebe Smith each wore a pistol and a gunbelt. Looking around, Lanham saw the rest of them did, too. He got a strong feeling they all knew how to use these pistols, and they would do it when the occasion came. On the Texas frontier, a boy didn't remain a boy long. Hardship made him into a man, or it buried him.

He stared at Joe Benson. "How come you here, boy? Your daddy know where you're at?"

"My daddy's been dead two years," Benson replied. "Since then I been up the trail twice with a cow outfit, all the way to the Kansas railroad."

Smith said, "Show him your arrow wound, Joe."

Benson put down his plate and rolled up his sleeve to

reveal a ragged scar. Lanham nodded soberly. "You're old enough. Glad you boys are in my dab."

Of all the men in the outfit, the captain himself looked the least fit. He sat to one side, picking at his food, his mind far away. He coughed occasionally, and his face paled. The nighttime ride to the Galindos', and then the return, had worn him to the bone.

Man like that, Lanham thought, *ought to be home in bed. Trouble comes, he won't be able to meet it.*

That, Lanham would find, was about as wrong as he had ever been.

Conversation with the young Rangers revealed that they had been sending out patrols for days, quietly searching the draws and valleys, the heavy brush and the scattered mottes for sign. "Captain's got him a spy system," Joe Benson confided. "Figures if the bandits work thataway, he can do it, too. One of them brought him a tip the other day. A bunch of us made a forced ride to the Rio Grande after a string of stolen stock and a passel of them bandits. We got there just as they rode out on the other bank. They hoorawed us a little and fired a few shots at us, but wasn't nothin' we could do. They got clean away, with the cattle, too."

"They were still in rifle range, wasn't they?"

"Law says we can't shoot across the river. Them, they don't bother about the law. They can do it and we can't. Odd thing, the way the law always seems to work out in favor of the lawbreaker and against the officer. Someday maybe they'll fix that."

During the next few days, because he had a better knowledge of the country than most of the Rangers, Lanham found himself being sent on patrol almost constantly. They would start before daylight and usually get in about dark. Whoever was in charge of each patrol would report to the captain that they hadn't come upon anything in particular. Yet all along, the captain knew raiding parties were working. Lanham could see the frustration building in him, and a sullen anger.

One day, off duty, Lanham saw a Mexican riding into camp on a gaunted horse. He was a lank, hunched figure of a man with straggly hair that hung down almost to his shoulders and a ragged beard that hadn't felt a comb. His eyes lit on Lanham a moment, and it was almost like being touched by a hot poker. Lanham felt his hair seem to rise on his neck. He'd never seen the man before, but instinctively he knew him. Old Sandoval. Jesús Sandoval, whose bony brown hands carried the stain of blood from more bandits than any man would ever know.

It was McNelly's rule that no one except members of the company rode into camp armed. Lanham figured Sandoval was going contrary to the rule, but he made no move to stop him. Something about the old Mexican made ice form in his veins.

He had heard the stories. Likely as not they weren't altogether true, but behind any smoke had to be some fire. Way the stories went, Sandoval once owned a small *rancho* on the Texas side of the river. Bandits from *el otro lado* raided his place and left his wife and daughter dead. Sandoval silently crossed the river carrying nothing but a gun, a knife and a heart twisted in hatred. By the time his identity was discovered and he was forced to retreat to the Texas side, he had sought out and butchered a majority of the men responsible. Now he hated all border jumpers. He lived only to spill the blood of bandits.

Odd, the name. *Jesús*. It was a common name in Mexico, for the people seemed to feel that only good could come for a child who carried the name of the Son of God. An ill-fitting name, though, for a man whose soul boiled with hate.

Lanham heard someone call, "Captain, here comes

Casoose." In English, following the Mexican border pronunciation, that was how the name sounded. Sandoval disappeared into the tent with the captain. Directly someone went to fetch coffee. It wasn't any of Lanham's business, but curiosity plagued him, and he watched the tent. The captain and Sandoval hunched over a map in animated conversation. He could see the dab leaders gathered close, anticipating orders but not breaching discipline by asking questions.

Presently the captain came out and called the men to order. He picked a detail, including Lanham. McNelly caught his favorite horse, a big King Ranch bay named Segal. Sandoval roped a fresh mount, a paint. Captain ordered extra cartridges for the Sharps rifles, to be placed in each man's saddlebags. On signal, Sandoval and a local scout named Rock led out, the captain behind them. The Rangers followed in a military column.

They rode hard that afternoon, pushing the horses almost to the limit of their endurance. Lanham could tell they were swinging toward Brownsville. After a long time the captain slowed, putting out two patrols, one on either side. The column moved slower then, and watchfully.

A while before dark, one of the patrols came back. Riding with them, sombrero brim flopping, was a Mexican prisoner. Lanham glanced at Sandoval. He saw the old *ranchero* straighten, his eyes on the prisoner the way a cat watches a mouse trapped in its paws.

One of the corporals saluted the captain, then jerked his thumb toward the captive. "Captain, we raised this 'un out yonder aways. Couldn't give a good account of himself. One of them bandits, we figure."

The captain had been lying down to rest. Lanham hadn't understood how a man in his frail condition could stand up to the ride he had made. Yet the captain did not look fatigued now. His stern eyes studied the captive.

With a jerk of his head, he signaled for Sandoval.

"Ask him who he is. Ask him what he's doing here."

A number of the Rangers including Lanham could have questioned the prisoner in competent Spanish, but none of them could do it in the chilling manner of Sandoval. The prisoner recoiled from him instinctively, fearing him on sight. The old *ranchero* asked a few questions, to which the captive gave ready but stammered answers.

"He lies, *capitán*," Sandoval said. "He says he is a rancher. He says he has a place over there." He pointed. "But I know all the people. He does not belong."

"Ask him where the bandits are, with the cattle they've stolen."

That was the first Lanham knew about their mission, though he had suspected it had to be something like this.

Sandoval translated the question. The way McNelly listened, Lanham figured the captain understood most of what was being said. But Sandoval was more than just an interpreter. The captive persisted in his story that he owned a small place *por allá*, and a few head of livestock, and that he knew nothing of bandits.

McNelly's eyes narrowed. "You still do not believe him, Casoose?"

Sandoval's long hair caught the wind as he shook his head. "He lies, *capitán*."

McNelly's eyes went hard. "Then reason with him. Your own way." McNelly walked back to the place where he had lain resting. Sandoval went to his paint horse and took his rope down. Lanham could see sweat break on the prisoner's face as Sandoval led him toward a tree, helped by one of the corporals. The old Mexican fitted his loop around the man's neck, tossed the end of it over a heavy limb, then pulled. Blood rose in the prisoner's face as his feet slowly cleared the ground. Sandoval held him there a moment, then let him down.

At the distance, Lanham could not hear the questions,

but he could tell Sandoval was talking, and the choking prisoner was answering him. Again the rope tightened, and the man's feet slowly cleared the ground. Sandoval held him a little longer this time.

The third time, the man was almost purple when Sandoval let him down. He crumpled, gasping, the words pouring out of him like a torrent as his breath began to come back. Sandoval and the corporal caught his arms and half supported him as they brought him back to the captain.

"His memory is better now, *capitán*."

Lanham's nerves tingled from watching. He turned to the sergeant. "I thought it was illegal to do a prisoner thataway."

"Old Casoose is the one who done it, and he never read a lawbook in his life. As for the rest of us, I didn't see a thing. Did you?"

"I reckon not, but it's a hard way to treat a man."

"It takes extreme measures, sometimes, to fit an extreme situation."

Almost eagerly now, the prisoner spilled all he knew. Lanham listened as the man described the raid the bandits had made, the cattle they had picked up, the route they were taking back to the river. With a stubby brown finger he pointed to places on McNelly's map. Among other things, he admitted he was a forward scout, making sure the way was clear.

"I knew it," the corporal muttered. "I could smell it soon's we saw him."

The captain made the prisoner go back over the story a second time, and then a third. He pressed for details, trying to trip him up. Finally he seemed satisfied. He had written down the names of the other raiders as the prisoner had given them to him. If they weren't caught today, they would go on the list for whatever time in the future they might fall into Ranger hands.

The prisoner looked relieved now that he had unburdened himself. He rubbed his neck, where Sandoval's rope had burned him. But there seemed a sense of security about him. The Brownsville jail never held the border bandits for long. They were always out on writ before the arresting officer could unsaddle his horse.

McNelly said, "Casoose, you know where to take this *hombre?*"

Sandoval nodded. *"Sí, capitán."* His jaw set hard, he motioned for the prisoner to mount his horse. At gunpoint, he took him away.

He'll be half the night getting the bandit to Brownsville and back, Lanham thought. But he didn't concern himself much. He lay down and stretched on the ground. He had already figured out that when a man rode with McNelly, he took his rest when and where the opportunity showed itself.

To his surprise, Sandoval rode back in about thirty minutes.

Alone.

Lanham glanced at the sergeant. "He couldn't of got to Brownsville in that time. He couldn't of . . ."

The thought stopped abruptly. He saw that much of Sandoval's rope was missing. Frayed ends showed where it had been freshly cut with a knife.

The sergeant said, "Captain couldn't afford to waste a man goin' to Brownsville. We couldn't be burdened with a prisoner on our hands on a forced ride. And we sure couldn't just turn him loose."

"Ain't there no other way?"

"You think of one?"

Lanham couldn't. But his stomach turned over.

Sixteen

NO FIRES, NO COFFEE. MEN RODE BETTER
on a lean stomach, McNelly said. Long before sunup,
the Rangers were in the saddle, riding steadily but not
pushing the horses hard as they moved across the salt
flats and the hardpan, through the marsh grass and
around the mottes of scrub oak. In the beginning ground
fog gradually burned away. Rock, up front, drew rein
and rode in a tight circle, leaning out of the saddle as
he studied the ground. He had found the trail.

"Pushed them through the night," he told the captain,
"figurin' on hittin' the river as soon as they can."

The captain was tense. "How far ahead of us?"

"Not far enough. We'll catch them."

"Lead out, then."

The scout struck a lope. Captain ordered the Rangers
into double file and followed. Nobody talked. Lanham
had been wishing for coffee, but now he forgot about it.
He felt excitement building in him and could see it in

the faces of the men around him as he turned in the saddle to look back. For a little bit, suspecting a battle lay ahead, he wondered what the hell he had let Captain talk him into joining this outfit for. But he decided he couldn't blame McNelly for it. The captain hadn't begged him.

Caught me in a weak moment, Lanham thought. *Looks more like a preacher than a fighter, and I always did have a weakness for a sermon.*

He saw Rock rein to a stop on a ground swell. The scout made a circular motion with his upraised hand, then dropped it and pointed. He had seen the bandits. Captain McNelly spurred up to the scout and took a spy glass from his saddlebags. Lanham didn't need the glass. He could see a herd of cattle far ahead, on the open prairie.

To the sergeant, Lanham said, "This is the Palo Alto Prairie. Oldtimers say the Mexican War started here, back in '45."

The sergeant's eyes were on McNelly. "There's fixin' to be another one now in just a little bit."

Across the open prairie, unhidden except for a scattering of salt cedar and Spanish dagger, the bandits milled excitedly.

"They're figurin' now," the sergeant said. "They're askin' themselves if they can make the river before we can get to them. But they can't."

"So they'll leave the cattle and run," Lanham speculated.

"Don't you bet on it. They're takin' count of us. Right now they probably figure we're Yankee troops out of Fort Brown, and up to now the troopers've been no match."

Lanham tried to count the riders, but the distance was too great. He guessed it was twenty or so. The bandits were pushing the cattle again. They had decided to bluff.

And if the bluff failed, they probably figured on making a fight of it with Yankee troopers.

They had a surprise coming.

The captain motioned for the Rangers to ride in close. His voice was not strong, but his eyes were like the muzzle end of a double-barreled shotgun. "Boys, you all know what we came down here·to do. So far, we've misfired on every shot. But today we're going to find out who runs the Nueces Strip—law or outlaw. Watch me for signals. I'll be easy for you to see; I'll be out front. Hold your fire. Don't shoot till I do. Don't scatter or get out of line. Fire straight ahead, or you'll shoot each other. Pick your man and don't let him go till he's dead. Any questions?"

There weren't any. When Captain spoke, there never were. He started the big bay down off the swell toward the Palo Alto Prairie, spurring Segal into a run. Heart quickening, Lanham leaned forward in the saddle and held his place in the column. The horses moved across the hardpan flat in a lope, hoofs shattering the crusted surface. Lanham dodged pieces of crust flung up by the horses in front of him.

Ahead lay an old riverbed of a type the Mexicans called a *resaca*. Left isolated when the river changed its course in some ancient time, it held a half-stagnant collection of rain and seep water. Seeing that a fight was coming, the bandits left the cattle and gathered in a fringe of brush at the far side of the *resaca*, waiting in confidence to repulse these brash *yanqui* soldiers who so foolishly challenged their right to other men's property.

Nearing the *resaca*, the captain slowed. He motioned for the Rangers to spread in a skirmish line. They moved out, right and left, spacing themselves about five paces apart. To the right lay a stretch of timber. McNelly signaled a lieutenant to take a few men and cut off any retreat in that direction. Then he rode out into the water.

Ahead, in the thin brush at the other side of the *resaca*, the bandits began to mill. Lanham decided they had probably figured out by now that these were not regular troopers. Sporadically the bandits began dropping a few shots at the Rangers. These plinked into the water, most of them short of the target. Lanham reached down for the rifle, remembered the captain's order and stopped his hand. His horse shied as a bullet kicked up a spray of water right in front of it.

Bandits or not, in a minute one of them is going to get lucky. Lanham brought the rifle up, wishing to hell the captain would fire that first shot. But McNelly sat straight in the saddle, eyes trained dead ahead, the horse wading.

Bandit fire became heavier as the outlaws realized this bunch of determined-looking men wouldn't turn around and go back. A horse screamed and went down thrashing. Its rider jerked his rifle from the scabbard, kicked his feet out of the stirrups and kept advancing afoot, the water up to his knees.

Sure as hell he'll start shooting now!

But the captain looked back only long enough to be sure the man was all right. He kept riding, still holding fire. Bullets kicked up water around the horses. Another mount went under, its rider cursing.

Suddenly one of the bandits broke and ran for his horse. Some of the others followed. But some stayed in the brush, firing. Lanham was sure he felt the hot kiss of a bullet as it went by his ear. His blood was racing now, his mouth so dry he couldn't have said a word. In his mind, though, he was shouting: *Captain, for God's sake . . .*

And finally McNelly raised his pistol and fired. He was so close to the outlaws now he could have chunked a rock into them. In the brush, a man cried out.

That was what the Rangers had waited for. Every outlaw who moved found himself a target, and the fire was deadly. Straight ahead of him, Lanham saw a man in a brown sombrero crouching in a clump of tall marsh grass. Lanham pulled the horse to a stop, raised the heavy Sharps and drew a bead. The recoil shoved him roughly backward, and the sound was like a cannon going off. He saw the man pitch forward across the grass, his bloodied sombrero rolling into the water.

Guns boomed on both sides of Lanham. He saw the flash of guns inside the brush and held his breath, expecting the smashing impact of a bullet.

Those bandits still on their feet after the first crackle of Ranger gunfire began retreating, running for their horses. The captain had one pinned down in front of him. McNelly called, "Somebody come help me. I'm out of shells."

At that the bandit jumped up and charged at him afoot, shouting in hatred at the *rinches apestozos*. It had been a ruse on Captain's part. He calmly leveled his pistol and shot the outlaw through the mouth.

A wounded bandit rose up out of the heavy grass almost directly in front of Lanham. In astonishment, Lanham looked at the beardless face of a Mexican boy who couldn't have been more than sixteen or so. He watched the boy raise a pistol, holding it with both hands because blood streamed from his right arm. He brought it to bear on Lanham. Lanham held the Sharps, but it had just as well have been a chunk of stovewood. He couldn't bring himself to fire.

Beside him, the sergeant's rifle boomed. The boy jerked backward, cut half in two.

"Your gun jam, Neal?" the sergeant asked quietly.

"No, *I* jammed."

The Rangers hit the brush. A sudden blast of gunfire ended the fighting there, though beyond the brush the escaping bandits spurred across the prairie in a disorderly rout.

Lanham found himself face to face with Captain McNelly. McNelly's eyes were narrowed and stern. "You had an outlaw in front of you, Neal. The sergeant had to shoot him for you. Why?"

"He was just a boy."

"He had a pistol on you. Boy or man, he was fixing to kill you. This is war. Next time, don't hesitate. Kill a man!"

The captain turned away. Lanham stared after him, his jaw set in anger. To the sergeant, he said, "That's the most cold-blooded son of a bitch that I ever saw."

The sergeant gave him a hard look. "It's a cold-blooded situation."

Somebody called, "Captain, I got one dyin' over here. He's callin' for a priest."

McNelly walked to the dying *bandido*. Solemnly he put away his pistol and took a Testament from his pocket. He removed his hat and read from the Book until the man's breathing stopped.

Lanham watched in surprise. The incongruity was too much for him. The sergeant said triumphantly, "Didn't know it all, did you, Neal? Didn't know Captain trained for the ministry, did you? War come along, or he'd of been behind some pulpit today, savin' souls in old Virginia."

Captain put his Testament away. He pointed south. "Some of them are trying to escape. Let's don't let them."

Enough outlaw horses were left in the ticket that the Rangers whose own mounts had taken wounds were able to find something to ride. They sprang into the big-horned, open-treed Mexican saddles and spurred across that broad expanse of hardpan. Fleeing outlaws with flagging horses found little to hide them. The straggling bandits jabbed big-roweled spurs into horses that had driven cattle all day yesterday and all last night. One by one, the Rangers overtook them. One by one, Ranger gunfire emptied the saddles. Some of the bandits lay on the ground and kept firing until they were literally shot to pieces. As each one was dispatched, the McNelly men spurred on again, after the others.

The long, running fight stretched over mile after mile of prairie. The sun was high when the final bandit rolled on the hardpan and went limp with one arm under him, legs doubled, eyes staring sightlessly into the sun. Almost before the dust settled, flies had found him.

McNelly signaled one of the Rangers to stop the run-away horse and bring it back. Lanham noticed a King Ranch Running W brand on it. That was one thing that gave the bandits an advantage all along: they were mounted on the best of stolen horseflesh.

McNelly leaned forward in the saddle and fell into a coughing spell. Lanham eyed him narrowly. *Damn wonder he's even here, a man no healthier than he is. By rights he ought to be lying back yonder with them bandits, dead of exhaustion.*

McNelly straightened his shoulders presently as if to show he could make another run if he had to. But his voice was weak. "Boys, you've done finely. Did any of them get away?"

The sergeant answered, "Not as I seen, Captain. Looks like we got them to the last man."

Lanham found himself strangely compelled to look at the corpse, against his will. "An ugly sight."

McNelly replied, "But long overdue. This is the first real blood drawn against Cortina's bandits. I intended it to be a total disaster."

Lanham watched the captain, wondering what held him up. He could see a flush in McNelly's normally pale face, a fire in his eyes. He knew then that excitement itself could act as a tonic. It could raise a man's blood like whisky, driving him beyond himself, beyond the limits of ordinary endurance. This same excitement had impelled Lanham. Now, the long chase over, a nauseous reaction began to set in upon him. The sick-sweet smell of blood brought him suddenly to a grave realization of what had happened here. He hadn't had time to comprehend fully that at least one man back yonder had died by Lanham's own hand—a living, breathing man, his brain smashed by a Sharps bullet as big as Lanham's thumb. The thought was instantly sobering.

Lanham's nervous fingers found a bullethole in his brush jacket. He stared, wondering when he had gotten it.

The exuberance of victory played high in the Rangers' young faces. They were brave, they were tough, they would do to ride the river with. They were too young to realize fully what they had done. And, maybe, thought Lanham, that was a blessing.

This kind of thing, he knew, could get in a man's blood like whisky. One finger still exploring the bullethole, he made up his mind it wasn't going to get in *his* blood. He'd stick with McNelly through whatever it took to see this thing to a finish; and then, by George, he was going to *quit*.

The shooting had drawn a couple of Mexican *rancheros* whose *adobes* lay at the edge of the prairie. They ventured out cautiously, taking their time. Sandoval rode over to investigate, found he knew them and brought them to McNelly.

"*A su servicio, capitán,*" said one, taking off his hat and bowing in the saddle. "Those were bad men. You did well."

The other said timidly, "I think perhaps some cattle of my brand were in the herd they stole. Would it be permissible, captain, for me to look?"

"After a while," the captain told them, using Sandoval

as interpreter. "First we need a cart or wagon to haul the bodies."

"*Sí, capitán,*" said the one who had asked about the cattle. "I shall go and bring it."

While the *ranchero* rode away, Sandoval and the other Mexican set to work bringing the bodies up into a straight line for the wagon. Lanham saw them tie a rope around a bandit's booted feet and drag him across the hardpan like timber being hauled to a campfire.

He turned quickly away. *Damn it, boys, I can't watch this.*

The Rangers fell into double file and moved at an easy trot back across the prairie toward the *resaca* where the shooting had started. Along the way they gathered the bandit's horses. A couple stood spraddle-legged, slowly bleeding to death from wounds. One was down. These the Rangers unsaddled, then shot, salvaging the gear.

After a while Lanham became aware of sporadic shooting, somewhere ahead. The captain reined up, listening, then swept his arm forward and moved into an easy, swinging lope. They came at length to a rush-filled, brackish pond. A Ranger stood shirtless beside a wounded sorrel horse. He had wrapped his shirt around the horse's neck to protect the wound from flies. As the riders approached, the Ranger pointed toward the pond and gave a signal for caution.

"Captain," he said, "we got a dead Ranger over yonder, and a bandit hemmed up in them rushes."

McNelly stiffened. "What Ranger?"

"Cebe Smith, sir. He's just a boy; he didn't know better. He got too close, and the bandit shot him."

Lanham shut his eyes. He heard Joe Benson cry out, for they had been friends.

Smith. A kid, that's all he was, a kid. But that's all most of them were. Wild, brave, gallant, foolish boys.

The Ranger said, "That snake is wounded, Captain. But he can still shoot."

Grimly the captain detailed the Rangers to surround the pond, being careful not to get opposite one another. On signal, several of them fired into the rushes. Lanham saw the tops of the rushes began to move as the bandit, in panic, sought safer ground. Rifles boomed. A groan came from the rushes, then a moment of thrashing, then quiet.

"All right, Casoose," the captain said, his eyes terrible, "you can fetch him out."

Seventeen

THEY RODE DOUBLE-FILE INTO BROWNS-
ville, Captain beside old Sandoval, leading them in.
Word of the battle had preceded them. People stood
almost shoulder-to-shoulder on both sides of the street.
Some looked in awe, some cheered, some watched in
silent curiosity. In many eyes Lanham saw stark hostility.
Many here were openly sympathetic to the red-beard
Cortina and his lusty bravos, for those were *hombres val-
ientes* who dared twist the tail of the yanqui ox, dared
spit in the *gringo*'s eye. The Texas Mexican people were
divided on the subject of Cortina's raiders. Many Mexicans had suffered as much or more than the *gringos*;
many had died at their hands. Yet many others had not
been victimized. To these this was a holy struggle, race
against race. To these people of the old blood, there was
no Texas south of the Nueces River. All this was still
morally part of Mexico, in spite of the lies on the *gringo*
maps. Two wars had not changed their minds. And if it

took bandits to fling the extranjeros back across the Nueces, then God go with the bandits.

Captain McNelly was keenly aware of the hostility. He dispatched a lieutenant to round up all patrols and bring them into town. They might be needed here more than in the brush.

An army officer rode toward the Rangers at the head of a small detachment of Negro troops. He brought his hand up in a sharp salute. "I'm Major Alexander, of Fort Brown. You, I take it, are McNelly?"

The captain returned the salute with only a nod, reserving himself till he knew how the wind blew. "I'm McNelly."

The major's stern expression gave way to a smile. "Congratulations, Captain. You've done what the army has wanted for months to do. Can I be of service?"

The captain relaxed a little. "Thank you, Major. I'd be pleased if you could send an ambulance out to Palo Alto Prairie and pick up a load of reformed bandits we left there. They gave us a little difficulty. They'll give you none."

"As good as done. Anything else?"

"I've got a couple of men with wounds. Nothing serious, but I'd appreciate it if your post surgeon could attend to them."

"I heard you suffered one fatality."

Captain nodded. "We'll want to bury him here."

"In the post cemetery. We'll give him full military honors."

Captain studied the major with a little of surprise. Evidently he hadn't expected much cooperation.

The major saw. "Captain, these border outlaws have spilled soldier blood. They enjoy shooting one of our Negro troopers almost as much as they like killing a *gringo* rancher. These men at the fort will stand behind anything you want to do."

"Enough to give my men a good feed? They've had nothing."

"Bring them on, Captain. They won't go hungry."

The post physician bound up the few wounds, and an ageless Negro cook fed the half-starved Rangers in a military mess hall. Lanham ate heartily and washed it down with enough coffee to drown a mule.

The army ambulance came in with its grim load. Major Alexander rode out with the captain and the Rangers to meet it. "They're your bandits, Captain," the major said. "What do you want to do with them?"

McNelly's eyes were like flint. "The town square. I want to haul them to the town square."

A sullen crowd followed the ambulance afoot. Lanham eyed them with uneasiness. They gestured angrily, shouting insults after the Rangers. To them, the men in the wagon were martyrs, slaughtered at the hands of Godless men who had stolen part of Mother Mexico.

It seemed to Lanham that McNelly deliberately set a slow pace as he pointed the way for the ambulance. At length he reined up on the plaza and pointed. "Right here. Stack them!"

The major blinked. "Stack them?"

"Right here. I want everybody to see. I want everybody to count them." His eyes held sparks as he looked at the gathering, threatening crowd. "I want them to get a good look and a good smell, and to know that these are just the first."

Grim-faced, young Joe Benson stepped down from his saddle. Other youthful Rangers pitched in to help him with the task. Lanham held back and let them, for this was a dirty job not to his liking. He felt a tug at the pit of his stomach as he watched them fling out the man he had killed in the brush at the edge of the *resaca*. The man had died with his eyes open, and those eyes seemed to look at Lanham.

He hadn't consciously kept a count, but as the last body hit the ground he found himself saying, "Sixteen."

Sandoval—who had enemies in the crowd and bluntly defied them by his presence—brought up a couple of acquaintances who began naming off the bandits whose bodies they could recognize.

"Camillo Lerma. *Coyote* Jiminez. Tellesforo Diaz. Guadalupe Espinosa. The *gringo* Ellis . . ." Sandoval grinned in perverse satisfaction. "*El Cheno*, he will be most unhappy, *Capitán*. These are some of his favorite *bravos*, some of the best thieves and throat-cutters in his command."

"Good," said McNelly. He turned to Sergeant Armstrong. "Put an eight-man guard on this plaza. Let the people come and look all they want to, but shoot any man who tries to move a body before I give the order. I want to be damned sure Cortina gets the word. I want to be sure everybody does."

Lanham was chosen for first guard. It was just as well. He couldn't have slept anyway, knowing what must be going on across the river in Matamoros, stronghold of Cortina and his violent band. He could imagine the fury that must be raging in the *cantinas*, fed now by tequila and mescal, and an inborn hatred of the *diablos Tejanos*.

Down on the Rio, the military had tied off the ferry to stop across-the-river traffic. Soldiers stood their posts up and down the bank, their worried eyes looking south toward the candlelit windows of Matamoros.

Joe Benson dropped down beside Lanham. He still seemed stunned by the loss of his friend. "You reckon they're a-hatchin' somethin' across yonder, Lanham?"

"It's a big town, damn sight bigger than Brownsville. They're strong enough to do just about anything they make up their minds to. Cortina came and took over this town once, back in '59. Folks say he raised a lot of

hell before the Mexican army talked him into goin'
home."

Even off duty, Lanham rested little. He sat watching
the plaza, half expecting a howling mob to burst into
the street, rescuing the bodies of the fallen raiders and
spilling *rinche* blood in these sands. They could do it if
they decided to; he had no doubt of that.

"I hope they come," said Joe Benson. "I'd love to get
a few of them for Cebe Smith."

"We already got them," Lanham pointed out. "Sixteen of them."

Joe was grim because of his loss, but Lanham per-
ceived exhilaration in the other young Rangers. They
met this situation with a boyish sense of high adventure
and patriotism, and a boundless faith in the captain.
Lanham knew that to most of them, as to many of the
Mexican people on the opposing side, this was primarily
a battle of race against race . . . that to them the enemy
here was as old as the Alamo.

It wasn't that way with McNelly. Whatever misgivings
Lanham had about him otherwise, he was convinced the
captain didn't take this as a war of white man against
brown. He had more perception than that. To McNelly,
as to Lanham, this was a contest of law against outlaw,
of order against disorder, right against wrong. If he was
merciless in pursuit of justice, it was not out of racial
motivations. He would be merciless anywhere in enforc-
ing what he considered to be the right.

Sitting there through the long night, Lanham let his
sleepless mind drift. Much of the time he thought of Zoe.
The memories brought him pain, and he would force
himself to think of the Galindo girl. But Zoe kept coming
back. It would have brought Zoe a savage satisfaction if
she could have seen this plaza, the outlaws lying dead
in the sand. Lanham was glad she couldn't.

Dawn came, and Lanham met it with burning eyes

red-tinged from lack of sleep. The captain came after daylight to relieve the guard. "Anything to report?" he asked Sergeant Armstrong.

"No, sir," the sergeant said, glad the long watch was over. "None of them bandits tried to get away."

"I think the message has been made clear now," McNelly said. "We'll leave the disposition of the bodies to Sheriff Brown. Mount up, boys. You'll have breakfast at the fort. Then we've got a Ranger to bury."

Word from across the river was that Cheno Cortina had paced his floor in a black fury all night, swearing vengeance with every breath. Rumor had it he wouldn't allow the Ranger to be buried in the ground he considered still a part of Mexico.

Major Alexander suggested, "Maybe it would hold down trouble if we got the funeral done quietly, and early, before anyone knows."

Captain McNelly's thin frame stood straight as a ramrod. "I *want* them to know. That boy died defying Cortina and his bandits. He'll not be buried like a coward."

So Private Cebe Smith defied Cortina to the edge of the grave. His flag-covered coffin was placed in a hearse. The Rangers lined up in double file behind the captain. Two full companies of U.S. regulars marched after the Rangers through the long streets of Brownsville, a tacit declaration that the troops at Fort Brown were in full support of McNelly. Every man was armed, for the river was no barrier if Cortina decided to send an army.

But the muddy Rio Grande ran quietly, undisturbed. At the military cemetery, men stood with heads bared as a bugle sent up a message that was part grief, part defiance. Across the river, Cortina must have heard it clearly.

But he had heard McNelly's message clearly, too.

Eighteen

IT WAS ONE THING FOR CORTINA TO
pace and rant in the luxury of his quarters, vowing revenge against McNelly. It was another for him to persuade hungry, *huarache*-shod volunteers to swim the river
and do the job. Those sixteen bodies gathering flies in
the Brownsville plaza had made an impression that no
number of official government protests and diplomatic
notes could ever do. The border simmered in suspense
and hatred, but few men dared make an opening move
on the *jefe*'s behalf. However intense their feeling against
McNelly, they respected him as a strong man on
horseback. Where raiding bands previously had often
numbered in the dozens of men, *el Cheno* found it difficult
now to get more than a few men to take the trail at a
time. They grabbed whatever they could find in a hurry
and fogged it for the river as if that *diablo* McNelly and
his fearsome *rinches* were right on their tails.

On both sides of the Rio, the story began to spread

that McNelly was something more than human, that he had strange powers, perhaps given him by the Devil himself in some Mephistophelian rite. Among those given to superstition, McNelly became a dread symbol of the omnipotent powers of Darkness.

He was not omnipotent; he was merely shrewd. Once before, McNelly had been on the river, carrying a special commission to study the border bandit problem and make a detailed report for the United States government . . . a report it filed away and did nothing about. The acquaintances he had made then stood him in good stead now. He began setting up a spy system, seeking out—through emissaries such as old Sandoval—those bandits whose loyalty to money was stronger than their loyalty to their chief. There were many of them. There always are. He located, too, honest citizens of both Mexico and Texas who were in a position to bring information and did so from a sense of right. Many who had hated the bandits had feared them too much to bear witness against them. Now, since Palo Alto, their courage began to rise.

If the situation on the border showed improvement, McNelly himself did not. The rigors of the campaign had fallen upon him with all their weight. He took a room at a hotel in Brownsville. He tried to ride out to the Ranger camp daily for inspection and to give orders, but he was gaunt and pale, and gradually his trips became less and less frequent. There was talk that the hotel people wanted him out, though they didn't have the nerve to tell him so. Plainly, Captain McNelly was a consumptive. No hotel man wanted a consumptive in his place; it scared other guests away.

McNelly would have scared them regardless.

His brain kept working, though his body was weak. His spy system continued to grow. And as it did, the wandering patrols had better and better luck cutting off bandit forays, for even from his sickbed McNelly was sending them where he knew the action would be.

The post physician checked on him regularly. Alarmed, he tried to persuade the Ranger officers to send for Mrs. McNelly, but none of them had the nerve to act without McNelly's orders, and they knew he wouldn't approve. So the doctor sent for her himself, asking no permission. He said: "I'm not in your command, McNelly. I can do what I damn well please."

They found an empty adobe house at the edge of town and moved the captain there. In the country, with his wife's cooking, he would have a better chance to recover . . . if recovery was in the cards.

Looking at him, Lanham Neal wondered. But he offered no comment. The captain lay on a cot in the shade of a huge cottonwood, watching his young son Rebel wrestling with a balky Mexican burro. Lanham said, "I believe you sent for me, Captain."

"Yes, Neal, I did. Sit down."

There was nothing to sit on but his heels, so Lanham squatted, careful not to let his big-roweled spurs gouge his rump. The captain asked him various questions about the scouts he had been on, the reports he was hearing. Lanham answered him matter-of-factly, sensing that wasn't what he had come for.

Presently Captain said, "I have a man here. I want you to identify him." He glanced toward the adobe house. "Casoose!"

Old Sandoval walked out from around the corner, flanked by a tall young Mexican. Lanham pushed quickly to his feet. "Vincente!"

Vincente de Zavala smiled and grasped Lanham's arms in an *abrazo*. "*Caporál!*"

Lanham stood off at arm's length and gave Vincente a careful look-over. The *vaquero* was leaner than when Lanham had last seen him. He bore a fresh knife scar on his cheek. But mostly what Lanham saw were his eyes. They seemed to have sunk back a little, and they carried the burned-in pain Lanham had become accustomed to in Sandoval's. "You've ridden some hard trails, *compadre*."

Vincente shrugged. "From what I hear, so have you."

Lanham turned to McNelly. "Whatever Vincente tells you, Captain, you can bet your money on. I'm tickled that he's back on this side of the river."

Vincente said, "I am not staying here, *caporál*. When it is dark, I will go back over. But now I work for you and *el capitán*, not just for me." He touched a hand to the Bowie knife on his belt. "They know the *capitán*. They do not know me."

A chill ran up Lanham's spine. They might not know Vincente, but they already knew of that blade.

The captain nodded in satisfaction. "That's all I needed you for, Neal. He came to me through Casoose. Said he had ridden with you. I just had to be sure."

"What if I hadn't identified him, Captain?"

McNelly's pale face did not change expression. "I'd have turned him over to Casoose."

Captain's orders had been for the men to stay out of trouble in Brownsville, but one night a few of them heard fiddle music in a Mexican danceroom and decided to take part in the *baile*. Words were exchanged, knives flashed and blood spilled on the floor. It added to the Rangers' reputation as fighters, which was perhaps a gain in some respects, but it ran against the captain's principles. When his men fought, he wanted it to be for something more substantial than dancing with a winsome *señorita*.

Captain McNelly got back on his feet. He put his wife and boy on the stagecoach for their home near Burton, saddled the big bay Segal and rode to the Ranger camp with a new set of orders. He was moving the company to Las Rucias, away from Brownsville's easy temptation to the Rangers and to those who hated them.

Some said hopefully that Captain was cured. Lanham could tell at a glance that he wasn't. McNelly was riding the river on borrowed time, and probably he knew it better than anybody.

At the new headquarters in Las Rucias cow camp, the McNelly spy system began paying dividends. Here his informants could be bolder. They could take a chance and ride straight into camp without worrying that they would be seen and reported by townspeople whose loyalty remained with Cortina. And the Rangers could move with more freedom from surveillance. More and more, the scouting parties were catching up with raiders on the Texas side instead of tracking them to the edge of the river and looking helplessly at them encamped on the opposite bank. After Palo Alto Prairie, those scattered small parties of bandits no longer tried to bluff it out to keep a stolen herd of cattle or a *remuda* of horses. At first sign of pressure, they abandoned their booty and spurred for the river. Sometimes they made it. Occasionally other Rangers waited there in ambush.

Cortina was feeling the pinch. Ships waited at the port of Brazos Santiago, past Matamoros, their holds ready for beef. Cortina had beef orders in his hands that would have meant a fortune, and these orders were going unfilled.

One day Lanham rode in with a scout detail after a long search upriver. It hadn't been a good scout. They hadn't seen anything but tracks. Lieutenant Robinson met Lanham at the corral.

"Neal, Captain wants to see you. You can eat later."

The urgency in his voice made Lanham forget that his stomach had growled at him the last thirty miles. He went straight to McNelly's tent. The captain lay on his cot, failing again. He shouldn't have sent Mrs. McNelly home. "Neal, I believe you're acquainted with a rancher by the name of Bailey? Andrew Bailey?"

Lanham's mouth hardened. "Yes, sir. I know him."

"We just got word there was trouble on his ranch. Bandits took a shot at him. Killed a woman instead."

It was as if McNelly had hit him on the head with the flat side of an ax. "A woman, sir?" He reached out for a chair and leaned on it to steady himself. "What woman?"

"Message didn't say." Compassion showed in the captain's eyes. "The girl you wounded at that Mexican place . . . would she likely have been with this Bailey?"

Lanham's voice dropped to a whisper. "I wouldn't be surprised."

The captain sat up, trying to keep pain from showing in his thin face. "Not much a person can do when his time comes . . . or *hers*. The Book says the day and the hour and the manner of our passing are written down at the moment we're born. So a man lives, and he tries to do his best, and he fights like hell when he's called upon because they can't kill him till his time comes. But when it comes, he'll die even if he tries to run.

"You better go to Bailey's, Neal. It's your place to do it. Take young Benson with you."

Lanham drank a cup of black coffee, stuffed some hardtack in his pockets and rode off on a fresh horse. It was all he could do to keep from running his horse to death . . . and Joe Benson's with it.

The boy protested after a while. "Lanham, you're spurrin' that horse like you hated him. Who you mad at?"

That brought Lanham back to earth. He realized the lad knew nothing about Zoe. He simply said, "I'm mad at *me*."

Zoe . . . Zoe . . . if it's Zoe, I'll . . . He clenched his teeth, knowing there was nothing he could do. *I oughtn't to've left her. I ought to've hog-tied her and taken her to Brownsville whether she liked it or not, instead of leaving her there with that land-hungry, woman-hungry Bailey.*

They hit Bailey's place at midafternoon. Lanham recognized a Mexican *vaquero* in the corral as one of those Bailey had sent to watch him and Zoe. "*Dónde está el patrón Bailey?*" he demanded.

The *vaquero*'s eyes were wide in astonishment. He pointed toward the house. "*A casa.* Why do you come here *señor? El patrón* will kill you."

"He can kill me," Lanham said, "just after he gets back from the moon." He reined the horse directly up to the house and swung to the ground. "Bailey!"

The wooden door moved inward. Bailey stepped out across the gallery, a rifle in his hand, pointed vaguely in Lanham's direction. He stared in surprise. "You remember what I told you I'd do, Neal, if ever you was to cross my sights?"

Lanham calculated his chances of drawing his pistol before Bailey could finish bringing that rifle into line. They were somewhat short. "You sent for Rangers."

Bailey blinked. "You're a Ranger? I don't see no badge."

"They never issued any. But you swing that rifle any farther around and I'll sure as hell prove it to you."

Bailey dropped the muzzle of the rifle. "I thought all you ever shot was women."

Lanham flinched, hating Bailey. "What about Zoe? We heard there was a woman killed."

"You never cared none for Zoe. You shot her yourself, remember?"

"I did my best not to; you know that. Now, damn you, tell me about Zoe before I ram that rifle down your throat."

A woman's voice came from inside the door. "What do you want to know?"

Lanham jerked his head around and saw her. "Zoe! You're all right?"

"Not altogether. I've still got a stiff arm. You'd know about that."

"We heard a woman was killed. I thought . . ."

Bailey said solemnly, "A woman *was* killed. My wife."

It took Lanham a minute to recover his wits. He stared first at Zoe, then at Bailey, feeling foolish. Finally he brought out, "Sorry. I know she was a good woman. I expect she was a real loss to you."

"A terrible loss," said Bailey. His voice betrayed him. Lanham could tell he didn't mean it. Suspicion already touching him, Lanham said, "Maybe you better tell us what happened."

Bailey laid the rifle against the wall and motioned for the two Rangers to come up onto the gallery and sit on a bench. His brow furrowed in pain that he obviously didn't feel. "Josefa'd been sick some lately. Zoe came here with me and my *vaqueros* after you shot her. I intended to have Josefa take care of her, but Zoe was takin' care of Josefa more than the other way around. She had one of them Mexican *curanderas* comin' over regular; thought somebody had cast a spell on her. You know all that stuff these people believe in. I tried to tell her it wasn't doin' no good. Yesterday I decided I'd just have to haul her into Brownsville to see a real white-man doctor. Four or five miles from the ranchhouse here, somebody took a shot at us from out of the brush. At *me*, I figure. They hit her instead. Killed her right off."

Lanham gazed intently into Bailey's face, looking for any sign that might betray the man as a liar. "Who did it?"

"Bandits. They got cause enough to want to kill me."

So have a lot of us, Lanham thought, glancing at Zoe. "See anybody?"

"No. I just wheeled the buckboard around and whipped the horses all the way home. Went back later with the *vaqueros,* but we couldn't find much of anything."

Lanham frowned. "I reckon we better look at the body."

Bailey said callously, "You'll need a shovel. She's under six foot of earth."

"You buried her without waitin' for an investigation?"

"Weather's hot, Ranger. You know that."

"Then you better show us the place where it happened."

Bailey shrugged. "Want to go, Zoe?"

Zoe looked at the floor. "No, I saw Josefa. I don't want to see where she died."

Bailey stepped down off the gallery. "I'll gather a few of the boys." Lanham watched him stride toward the barn, then brought his gaze to Zoe. He found her still looking at the floor. He wished he knew some proper words to say. "I been thinkin' about you an awful lot."

"I think about you, too . . . every time my arm starts to hurt."

Lanham bit his lip. "I been hopin' you'd realize there wasn't nothin' else I could do. I wouldn't of hurt you for the world."

"Not even for that dark-eyed Mexican girl?"

Lanham shook his head. "You still goin' to stay here now that Bailey's wife is gone?"

"Why not? He'll need somebody."

"People will talk."

"I stayed with *you* once, remember? We just let them talk."

Whipped, Lanham walked down to his horse. Joe

Benson followed, boiling with questions he knew better than to ask.

Bailey headed them out the wagon road. After a while he reined up and pointed. "Right there. That's where we was. And yonder . . . yonder in the brush is where the shot come from."

The brush didn't appear very thick to Lanham. "Looks like to me you could've seen a man in there."

"With a dead woman and two boogered horses on my hands? I didn't do much lookin'. Not till later, when I come back with the boys."

"Find tracks?"

"You always find tracks in this country. All the tracks you want. Trouble is, they don't tell you much."

They can tell you if you want to know, Lanham thought. He rode over to the place where Bailey said the shot came from. He found it hopeless. Bailey's *vaqueros* had ridden around here so much that if there had been any tracks, they were lost in a tangled maze.

Bailey sat with legs braced in the stirrups, hands pushing against the pommel of the saddle, stretching himself. He did not look bereaved. "Well, Neal, what do you think?"

Lanham saw no reason to dodge it. "I think you're a damned liar. I think you're a murderer. I think you went and killed her yourself."

Color surged into Bailey's face. He instinctively reached for his pistol but caught himself.

Lanham went on, "You already had all you wanted from your wife . . . her land. Now there was another woman with good looks, and land, too . . . Zoe. You took advantage of the bandit trouble to get rid of the old one. She didn't have anything more to give you anyway. You rigged the whole thing."

"No, Neal. I had to take her to a doctor. She was sick . . ."

"Sick with seein' and knowin' what was goin' on in your mind. You think a Mexican woman's not just as smart as any other? She saw through you better than Zoe did. She knew you didn't have Zoe here just to protect her. She knew you wanted Zoe and that sooner or later you'd have her. No wonder that poor woman was sick. No wonder she had a *curandera* tryin' to break a spell. You're the one put the spell on her, like you're puttin' it on Zoe."

"You're crazy, Neal." Bailey glanced at Joe Benson. "Can't you tell he's crazy?"

Lanham said, "I may have some of the details wrong, but I'd bet everything I own—which ain't much—that I got most of it pegged."

"Is that what you're goin' to tell your Captain McNelly?"

"You bet you."

"Even if it was true, you couldn't prove it."

"No, Bailey, that's the hell of the thing. I can't prove it."

Bailey went a little easier. "What you figure on tellin' Zoe?"

"Nothin'. She wouldn't believe me if I did."

Bailey gained confidence. "You're right. If you was to tell her the sun would come up tomorrow out of the east, she'd look for it in the west. She hates you, Neal. Same as I do. If you wasn't a Ranger, and if I didn't know that crazy captain you've got would come and wipe us out to the last man, I'd kill you right where you're at."

Lanham felt a fury rising that would go out of his control if he didn't get away from here. "I won't always be a Ranger, Bailey."

"When you're not, come back. Then I'll kill you."

"Maybe you'll *try*." Lanham jerked his head at Joe Benson. "Come on, button. Let's get out of here."

*   *   *

He found himself riding a familiar trail, going back. He didn't take the direct route he had used coming out. Joe rode alongside him patiently, his eyes asking questions. Lanham didn't volunteer him any answers until they rode into a ranch yard.

Joe said, "Looks deserted. What place is this?"

"Belongs to Zoe Daingerfield, the woman at Bailey's."

What Joe didn't know, he guessed at. He said simply, "Oh."

Lanham didn't dismount. He sat there, gaze slowly covering the yard, holding a bit on the empty *jacal* he and the *vaqueros* had built for Zoe.

Joe finally said, "My old daddy told me that a sore never heals if you keep pickin' at it."

Lanham scowled but let it pass. "Come on, we're wastin' time."

He knew another trail, and he took it, too. Joe said, "I thought camp was yonderway."

"It is. But we're goin' thisaway."

He rode out of the brush and into the clearing where the Galindo *rancho* lay. Relief came as he saw that the shack still stood, just as he had last seen it. He had half thought Bailey or Zoe might have come back and burned it.

Captain's orders about such things seemed to have taken hold.

Galindo children scattered like chickens, until they recognized Lanham and knew it was all right. They edged back cautiously. *Señora* Galindo came out, saw who it was and broke into a broad smile. But Lanham didn't see it, particularly. He was looking for the girl. In a moment she stepped out the door, trying to straighten her hair.

"*Señor* Neal," she smiled. "We are blessed by your presence."

Joe Benson stared, open-mouthed. "What's that she said, Lanham? What's that she said?"

Lanham translated for him. He told the girl, "I have been wondering if you were all right. Have you been bothered by anyone?"

"We are fine, *señor*. No one has come to bother us. We are grateful to you for that."

Joe had to know what she was saying. Lanham told him, then added, "You ought to learn to speak Mexican."

Joe nodded. "I believe I will."

Señora Galindo asked them to stay and she would see what she could find for the Rangers to eat. Joe was for it, but Lanham told him in English so the women couldn't understand, "You can see they got very little. Anything we eat is that much taken away from the kids."

He lied that they had already eaten. Lanham looked at the girl, measuring her against Zoe, wishing this girl could make him stop thinking about the woman he had lost. She got prettier every time he saw her, seemed like. Maybe that was because he was hungry. If he played his hand halfway right, he figured he could have her.

But he knew, looking at her, that it wouldn't work. She was still a girl, and a girl wasn't enough, not after Zoe. Zoe was a *woman*.

He took off his hat and said his *hasta luegos* and rode away, knowing there was no use in coming this way anymore.

Joe Benson kept looking back. "By George, Lanham, I do believe that's the prettiest Mexican girl I ever seen. Maybe the prettiest girl of any kind I ever seen. You got a claim on her?"

"No claim."

"Would it be all right with you if—sayin' my duties was to bring me thisaway again—if I was to stop off and visit with her some? Now, I don't mean for any bad purpose, nothin' like that. Not with that kind of a girl. I mean just to talk with her."

"You'd have to learn Mexican."

"I'd learn it. I'm tellin' you, Lanham, I'd sure learn it."

Lanham came very near to smiling, for a minute. "I'd have no objection atall. I think it'd be a dandy idea."

Nineteen

CAPTAIN MCNELLY WAS DUBIOUS. "YOU have a lot of reason to dislike Bailey. Maybe you're letting that color your opinion."

"My opinion is worse than I could tell you, Captain."

"You still couldn't prove anything."

"No, sir."

"Sooner or later, fate always overtakes a man like that. He'll make a mistake one day. Right now we have border bandits to worry about."

Word from spies across the river indicated that Cortina was getting desperate to meet those lucrative beef contracts. He had stepped up his encouragement to his followers. After all, those *gringos* were on land stolen from your fathers and grandfathers, he argued, and those are grandmother's cattle. Who has a better right? Cortina upped his paying price for stolen beef to twelve dollars a head. That was enough to start some hesitant *bravos* trying their luck again. The Rangers stopped some, but with 150 or 200 miles of the Rio Grande to cover, the thirty-man McNelly force couldn't hope to catch them all.

Despite sporadic Ranger successes, Lanham could tell the captain was becoming more and more restless over the many bandits they never even saw, the ones they knew about only by the tracks on the muddy banks of the river, and by the reports of murdered *vaqueros* and stolen livestock that drifted down from the north.

The gray of his sickness was coming over Captain again. Lanham knew someone ought to send for Mrs. McNelly, but the army doctor wasn't here now. Any Ranger who dared could toss his commission in the river.

Ailing, the captain still didn't divulge his plans. But times when he felt like it, he began talking to the men. Times, he allowed himself to get closer to them than he ever had before.

He knows his days are numbered, Lanham thought.

Captain would talk of his guerrilla days in Confederate service in Louisiana, or he would talk of religion, a subject on which he was exceptionally well versed. Lanham had seen brutality in the man, but he remembered there had been brutality in the Bible, by men favored of God. Like these, perhaps, McNelly was convinced he worked in a righteous cause.

Once, while Lanham was resting between scouts, he heard the captain give his appraisal of what it would take to clean up the border for good and all. "War!" McNelly said. "A war would put a stop to the raiding. I'm afraid nothing else will. The soldiers, they try, but they're tied down by red tape and foolish rules. That bunch in Washington is afraid they'll hurt Mexico's feelings, so they won't let a soldier cross the river, even in hot pursuit. Cortina knows this, and he takes advantage of it.

"Down in Mexico City, they've got too many troubles of their own. They've got revolutions on their hands. They can't be worried about one tin-pot border politician. They could put a stop to Cortina in a hurry if they put their minds to it. And war with this country would *put* their minds to it, you can bet. Let our government move troops into Mexico and the *politicos* in Mexico City would come awake in a minute. They don't want to fight the United States."

Lieutenant Robinson, late of Virginia, said, "But the United States doesn't want to fight them, either, Captain. So it's just not going to happen."

"You never can tell, Lieutenant." McNelly had a scheming look in his eyes. "You never can tell."

Summer gave way to fall, and raids continued, though still not on the scale they had been before Palo Alto Prairie. Captain rode when he could. More often, he had to lie in camp. Two or three times Lanham found Vincente de Zavala there, delivering information. Usually when Vincente brought word, bandits died.

With spies, there was always the risk that sooner or later one would light both ends of the candle. In the end it was not a Mexican who betrayed McNelly . . . it was a *gringo* renegade he had come to trust. This spy parleyed a long time. When the captain came out of his tent, he told the men to get ready to move. On McNelly's orders, the camp cook fed them hardtack, beans and coffee.

Lanham knew what that meant: a long, hard ride. They rode east, which surprised him, because most of the raids had been to the west. After a long time they angled north. Captain knew where he was going, but he didn't confide. He just kept riding, right into the teeth of a Texas norther. Without food—without so much as coffee—they pulled up at last in a large thicket and sat down to wait for what the *gringo* spy had told the captain was coming.

Nothing happened the first day. Captain sent scouts out to patrol, but they found nothing. The company waited wet and cold, bellies empty. The captain himself finally rode out for a *pasear*, though he looked too sick to do it. He came back empty-handed.

Four days they waited in ambush. The raiders never appeared. And at last old Casoose, out on a one-man circle, came in with a galling report. It had been a ruse. The captain's spy had taken a payoff to lure the Rangers out of the way. Then raiders by the dozens had crossed the Rio Grande from an upriver stronghold, Rancho Las Cuevas. They had looted and burned ranchhouses and stores, slaughtered *vaqueros* where they found them, gathered uncounted horses and perhaps eight hundred cattle.

Lying cold in his wet blankets, Captain had been sick even before Sandoval came back. Now, as he listened, his thin face was almost blue. The spirit seemed gone from him. He had taken a licking, the worst licking of his life. It was obvious he would die if he stayed here this way. Sick at heart as well as of lung, McNelly turned the command over to Lieutenant Robinson and rode north to seek recuperation in the warmth of his own house, the good air of his farm, the tender care of a loving wife.

Along the border the word quickly spread that McNelly was gone. His enemies said he had been whipped and had run out like a dog, tail between his legs. Others said he was dying, that he would never come back.

When Lanham Neal watched Captain ride off on Segal, thin shoulders hunched against the cold, he had a strong feeling he would never see McNelly again. His throat tightened, and his eyes burned. Smoke from that damned fire, he thought.

Sure, McNelly had some things about him that were hard to accept. He could be ruthless when there was a

176   Elmer Kelton

need for it. Turning prisoners over to Casoose was the
thing that stuck most in Lanham's craw. But what Casoose did to the bandits was no worse than what the
bandits did to those *gringo* cowboys or Mexican *vaqueros*
or store clerks who fell into their hands, and particularly
any comely young women who might strike a border
jumper's fancy. Hell, it was a war whether they chose to
call it one or not.

One thing always in McNelly's favor was the blanket
order he had given his Rangers from the first, "Leave
the law-abiding citizens alone. Don't kill a beef, don't
even kill a chicken, unless a man gives it to you, or unless
you pay him for it. Go hungry if you have to, but leave
the honest man's stock alone. Go into a house only if a
man invites you to. Sit down only when he says so.
Whether he be *gringo* or Mexican—black, brown or
white—if he's done no wrong, molest him in no way.
We're after outlaws, nothing else."

Well, Lanham thought, *he's been whipped. But it wasn't
Cortina that did it; it was lung fever. No man alive is big enough
to bring the captain down.*

The Rangers tried after the captain left, but it just wasn't
the same. The officers were less certain of what to do.
Emboldened, the *Cortinistas* returned to raiding on their
old scale, and this brought fear back to many of the
people who had cooperated with McNelly. The spy system disintegrated. Palo Alto Prairie had been a flash in
the pan, some were saying. Pure luck, and nothing else.
The captain had been a failure, and the Rangers were
a farce.

It was an unhappy camp at Las Rucias. Lanham Neal
was glad to be out on scout as much as he could, not
that being on scout meant much in the way of results.
Sure, they killed an outlaw now and again, but it didn't

seem to discourage anybody. What was a man when beef had jumped to eighteen dollars a head?

One cold day Lanham rode in from a wasted scout and found a chunky, sad-faced Mexican *vaquero* hunched at the campfire, disconsolately waiting. "Bonifacio, *como le va?*"

Bonifacio stood up. "*Caporál*, it is good to see you."

"If it's good, why don't you smile a little bit? You look like you'd been to a funeral."

Bonifacio shrugged. "I have come to talk to you about *la patrona.*"

"Zoe?" Lanham frowned. "What happened to her?"

"Nothing. Not yet. But perhaps soon."

"What's *goin'* to happen to her?"

"The Bailey, he says he will marry with her."

Lanham turned away so Bonifacio couldn't see his face. "His wife's not hardly even cold in her grave." He grimaced. "What does Zoe say?"

"She says nothing, *caporál.*"

"She look happy?"

"She has not looked happy in all this time."

"She send you to fetch me?"

Bonifacio shook his head. "She does not know I am here."

"She made any sign she don't want to get married to Bailey?"

"No sign. It is something I feel. I think you should come to see about her, *caporál.*"

Lanham got a cup of coffee and sat beside Bonifacio, staring into the fire, pondering a long time. "Never did seem like I could bring her any luck. If I was to ride over there now, I'd probably kill Bailey, or he'd kill me. Either way, she'd suffer for it."

"You don't help her?"

"If I knew a way. But like you said, she didn't send for me. She ain't said she don't want to marry Bailey.

She's a grown woman, Bonifacio. I got no claim."

"That Bailey is *un mal hombre*, mean as a Comanche. It is said among the *vaqueros* that he killed his wife."

"Is there any proof?"

"Nobody saw. But they whisper it, when he cannot hear."

"If there's no proof, there's not a thing we can do."

"Amigo . . ." Bonifacio paused. "If he has killed one wife, might he not someday also kill another?"

Lanham let the cup sag. The coffee spilled. "Bonifacio, quick as you get the chance, ask her if she wants me to come and get her. If she says yes, come tell me and I'll be there faster than a man ever rode. If you don't come back, I'll figure she said no."

"She will not ask for you. She is a woman of pride."

"But a *woman* . . . old enough to make up her own mind."

Bonifacio rode away as discouraged as when he came. Lanham watched for him the next day, and the day after that. When the fourth day passed, he knew the *vaquero* was not coming. Somehow Lanham had known he wouldn't. But somehow, also, he was bitterly disappointed.

Twenty

NOVEMBER CAME, AND COLD WINDS drove down from the northern prairies across the hill country of Central Texas and on to the coastal plains and the desert lands below the Nueces. Without Mc-Nelly, the little company of Rangers stayed encamped at Las Rucias, making half-hearted scouts up and down the river, occasionally running into *Cortinistas* but most often just finding where they had been. When they took a prisoner, the Rangers would send an escort with him to Brownsville. Usually the man was out on bond before the Rangers finished scribbling their report in the sheriff's office.

It suited the sheriff's jealous staff. "You Rangers been too high and mighty," a deputy snarled at Lanham. "I'm glad to see you bulldogs wearin' a muzzle."

The Rangers wouldn't turn any prisoners over to Casoose, not since the day he had tied two of them to a tree by their necks and to a saddle horse by their feet and had whipped the horse away. Even fanatic old San-doval wouldn't have done a stunt like that if McNelly had been there. McNelly believed summary execution had its place, but cat-and-mouse games did not.

Discouraged, half expecting disbandment orders from Austin any day, afraid the captain would die without ever coming back, some of the Rangers began talking about going home. Some talked of hunting cowboy jobs in the Nueces Strip, but winter was a bad time to be out of work, for not many ranches would be hiring now till spring. With the Rangers there was the promise of reg-ular pay, at least until Austin decided the McNelly com-pany was no longer of service. It wouldn't bother the legislature to leave a bunch of men stranded down on the river in the middle of winter. They weren't running a charity ward.

Lanham Neal had about made up his mind to strike out for the Texas Panhandle and new country. Folks were saying McKenzie and the army had coraled the Comanches, and now cattle herds were venturing into that vast tableland. Maybe there'd be work up there for a cowboy. If he couldn't find a job, perhaps he could hunt buffalo the rest of the winter. One thing sure, he didn't want to stay down here in the Strip anymore, once he left the Rangers. Bonifacio had brought him the news when Zoe Daingerfield married Andrew Bailey. Well, that was a door slammed for good. Nothing here to hold Lanham anymore. Sooner he wiped the river mud off of his boots, the better.

He particularly wanted to leave after the appalling day Vincente de Zavala and Casoose led a patrol toward a thin column of dark smoke. They found a small Mexican *ranchito* lying in black ruins, the *ranchero* hanging in his own brush arbor, his wife dying of bullet wounds, several small children crying in terror.

"*Mi hija*," the woman gasped. "They took my daughter."

The Rangers spurred out, following the tracks of the *ranchero*'s pitifully small herd. They hauled up at the bank of the river, too late as usual. Lanham's heart sagged as he saw a tiny figure lying silent and still, like a crumpled rag doll. Dismounting, he gently turned the girl over. He recoiled at the sight of the knife plunged into her breast.

Joe Benson cursed softly. "Why couldn't they have let her go? Why'd they have to kill her?"

Lanham shook his head. "She might've done this herself." He looked across the river, gritting his teeth. "Patriots!"

Old Casoose Sandoval knelt by the girl, the tears flowing unashamedly down his leathery brown cheeks and into the tattered beard. He began a cry that was half a moan, half a curse. He was remembering another time, another girl.

In bitter frustration Lanham said, "Nothin' more we can do here. Nothin' but take her home."

Old Sandoval grasped the knife and pulled it out. He wiped what blood he could onto the girl's torn dress. From his pocket he took a whetstone and began to work on the blade. Madness was in his eyes. "*Amigos,*" he said, "tell the lieutenant I will be back in my own time. I go across the river."

Lanham had no inclination to stop him. "Go ahead, Casoose."

Vincente de Zavala put his hand on the scout's thin shoulder. A little of the madness was in his eyes, too. "I go with you, old man."

Riding away, the Rangers carried the girl across Joe Benson's saddle, and Joe rode behind Lanham. Joe kept looking back toward the luckless girl. "Lord, Lanham, I wisht the captain was back."

Lanham shook his head. "Forget it, Joe. I doubt we'll ever see him again."

He was wrong. One afternoon a soldier from the United States cavalry detail at Edinburg galloped into Las Rucias camp with a telegraph message just received over military lines. Lieutenant Robinson gave a whoop. "It's Captain! He's at Ringgold Barracks!" The Rangers cheered.

Ringgold! Lanham had never been there, but he knew it was upriver at Rio Grande City.

"Says for us to get the hell down there as fast as we can ride. He'll meet us at Las Cuevas crossing. We're goin' after bandits!"

Old Casoose led the way, ducking and dodging through the tangles of brush, setting a hard pace, licking his cracked lips in anticipation. A wild new enthusiasm fired the young Rangers now. Gone was the black discouragement of the last long weeks. Captain was waiting at Las Cuevas! A new deck of cards was about to be dealt.

It was one of the fastest forced rides in the history of the Texas Rangers—fifty-five miles in something like five hours. Shortly after dark, the entire company reined up at the bank of the Rio Grande, horses lathered and winded, so tired they trembled and let their heads sag. It was a wonder half of them hadn't died.

There stood Captain, his face thin and colorless but his clothes fresh, his beard trimmed, his eyes a-flash with the fire of old. Like a dying candle, Captain would flare brightly before life snuffed out.

Behind him waited a young army officer and a sizable company of U.S. troops. Captain shook hands with his own officers, glowing in pleasure. "Boys, it's good to see you; mighty good. How've things been?"

Lieutenant Robinson answered obliquely. "They'll be

better, Captain, now that you're back. Just tell us what you want us to do."

Not that Captain wouldn't. McNelly took the black cigar from his mouth and used it to point at the river. "Boys, they're testing us. Word from our spies is that Cortina has got an order for up to eighteen thousand head of beef. To get that many he'll have to amass a small army and make a sweep over the whole Nueces Strip. They've just finished a raid of sorts, feeling us out, seeing if they can get away with it. And they *did* get away with it, up to now. You can see their trail." He pointed to a mass of cattle and horse tracks, spread like a muddy blanket over the river bank, disappearing in the murky water.

"Boys, across yonder, back from the river aways, lies Rancho Las Cuevas. You've heard of it. It's the biggest den of border bandits west of Matamoros. It's the stronghold of old Juan Flores Salinas, and he's one of the biggest chieftains Cortina has. A few hours ago, those Cuevian bandits crossed something like 250 Texas cattle right here. A Mexican lookout got word to the army, but by the time the troops could get here it was too late. The *Cortinistas* had the cattle across the river. They fired some shots. They knew the soldiers wouldn't fire back. Outlaws can ignore international law. Soldiers can't . . . at least, they don't."

"Boys, that river has stopped us once too often. If they get away with this one—and they think they already have—they'll be back here in force for the biggest raid since Santa Anna. A lot of good people in Texas will die . . . *gringos* . . . Mexicans . . . all kinds. Now, they've got those stolen cattle in corrals over yonder. One of our spies has already looked."

He pointed, and Lanham Neal recognized a grim Vincente de Zavala.

"I'm going over there," Captain said matter-of-factly.

"I'm going to get those cattle and bring them back. I'd like all the help I can get, but I'll not order a man to go. Every man who crosses the river with me will be a volunteer."

The men looked at each other, weighing the danger. Captain said, "I can't guarantee you'll come back. I can't guarantee you anything but a damned good fight. Any of you who want to go, step up."

Lanham waited to see how many others would go. He didn't intend to swim across there with nobody but the captain. One of the reasons for McNelly's recklessness was his firm belief in predestination—that a man couldn't be killed until it came his appointed time to die. Lanham did not share the comfort of that belief. One after another, the Rangers stepped forward. Lanham went with them.

The captain nodded, pleased. "Good. We'll take time to fix some supper, then. We've got an old rowboat tied up here on the bank. It's leaky, but it'll make it across. We'll start putting you over after midnight, when the *Cortinistas* have given us up and gone to sleep."

While they waited, more troopers arrived. The soldiers had tied into the military wire that followed the river from Ringgold Barracks to Fort Brown. An operator was tapping out messages for McNelly as well as for the army officers. Word came that Major Alexander was on his way from Fort Brown with a Gatling gun.

Lanham could tell by the stars when it was midnight. He hadn't slept. Captain moved to rouse his Rangers, but he found them already waiting. He asked one of the army lieutenants, "You coming with us?"

"I want to," the officer said, "but I have to wait for the wire to bring me orders."

Vincente de Zavala stood ready. Captain shook his head. "I can't let you go, *amigo*. My Rangers all know old Casoose. Most of them don't know you as well. In the dark they might make a mistake."

Vincente seemed inclined to argue, but nobody argued long with Captain. Vincente stepped back and faced Lanham Neal. "*Caporál*, you know what is across that river?"

Lanham said, "Never been there."

"Three hundred, maybe four hundred *bandidos* and Rancho Las Cuevas. How many *rinches* does our captain have?"

Lanham swallowed. "Not near enough."

Sergeant Armstrong overheard. "Ten to one ain't no odds for Captain. Anybody ever tell you about the time Captain took forty men and captured eight hundred federals over by New Orleans? Trotted his men out in sight time and again, here one time, yonder the next . . . convinced the Yankees they was surrounded by a force twice their size. They just laid down and give up."

"You think he can do it again here?"

The sergeant shrugged. "I just let Captain do the worryin'."

Lanham thought, *I expect I'll help him worry a little.*

Captain went over on the boat's first trip, taking the lead as always. Presently the boat was back for three more. Lanham had to sit and wait, and the waiting was not good. It gave him too much time to wonder if the captain really had a plan or if the fever had robbed him of reason. *Ten to one.* Lanham figured it six ways from Sunday, and it still came out impossible.

Casoose and four others tried swimming their horses across. On his next return, the boatman brought an order from the captain that no more horses be brought. They had all but gone down in treacherous quicksand on the far bank. This operation would be carried out afoot. In Lanham's view this only lengthened the odds. But he wasn't the captain.

Early-morning fog had settled in wet and heavy by the time the last Rangers made it to the Mexico side. Captain asked one of the men anxiously, "Any word from the military?"

"They're still waitin' for orders, Captain."

"They'll wait till hell freezes over, then," Captain said in frustration. "If they haven't been given orders by now, they never will be. We'll do it by ourselves." He pointed to a cattle trail that led up the bank and into the dense fog. "The horsemen will lead out."

Casoose was more or less familiar with the land, so he rode in front, walking his horse. The trail through the mesquite and willows and sacahuiste was too narrow for a double file. The men strung out.

Lanham was a cowboy and not used to walking. His feet ached before he had traveled far. They ached a lot more before the Rangers finally hauled up at a fence which had wooden bars for a gate. Ground fog still clung thick and heavy, so that at times, even in the spreading light of dawn, the Rangers had not been able to see each other all the way from the head of the line to the rear. Captain ordered the men up close.

"Boys, we're at Rancho Las Cuevas. You all know what we're up against, but we've got surprise in our favor, and the fog. We'll hit them hard and fast. Kill everybody you see except women and children. They're all *Cortinistas*, gathering to raid Texas. I'm counting on them not knowing how many of us there really are. If we hit them hard enough, they'll figure it's an army. Don't hesitate. When you see a man, shoot. All right, Casoose, let down the bars."

The Rangers passed through the gate and immediately spread out into a skirmish line. Lanham saw the broad form of sheds and other out-buildings. Ahead, he could hear the sound of axes, chopping firewood for breakfast.

A man shouted, "*Quién vive?*" He fired one shot. A Ranger rifle roared, and the sentry went down. At that, Casoose gave a wild yell that made Lanham's hair stand on end, and he spurred his horse forward. The Rangers broke into a trot, shouting.

Woodchoppers started throwing their axes aside and running for their guns. One stood foolishly staring, bewildered. He went down as if struck by his own ax. Ranger rifles and pistols cracked in the dawn. One after another, the sentries and woodcutters fell. Out of a long building, men came running, fumbling sleepily with their buttons, peering through the fog. A few fired wildly, but most never lived long enough to trigger a shot.

In moments the shooting was over. Across the broad yard Lanham saw bodies crumpled, many of them not dressed. Not one was a Ranger.

The Texans paused for breath, watching for more men to pour out of these buildings.

Lanham felt a stab of misgiving. Vincente had said three or four hundred men. There wasn't room for that many. He had seen a dozen or so at most. Something was terribly wrong.

Casoose knew the answer. "*Capitán!* In this fog, we have made a mistake. This is not the Rancho Las Cuevas. This is Las Cachuttas. It is an outpost, only."

Captain stood stiff, dismayed. "Where *is* Rancho Las Cuevas?"

Casoose pointed, "*Poco mas allá.* Maybeso half a mile."

Captain was not a cursing man, but had he been, he would have scourged the heavens. "They're bound to have heard the shooting. They'll be ready for us now. But maybe they'll be cautious about meeting us. They don't know how many we are. Boys, we're going on."

They made the half mile in a hard trot, Lanham's feet still hurting. The fog was thinning some but still provided cover. The sand caused heavy running, and the brush was thick and clutching. Any moment Lanham expected a whole Mexican army to come bursting through that fog, guns blazing. The Rangers wouldn't last long enough to unshuck a *tamali*.

Up front, Casoose topped a rise and signaled. Captain immediately ordered the men to fan out. Lanham moved forward cautiously, not in any hurry to look.

Ahead of them and down a little, the *rancho* lay like a small village in a dish-like opening, its sides enclosed by a stockade fence of upright poles. Down in the corrals, Lanham could see a flurry of activity. The *Cortinistas* were saddling their horses, some already done and shouting for the others to hurry. Many seemed to be fumbling along. Lanham realized they must have celebrated last night, enjoying the success of their raid across the river, anticipating greater glory to come. Mescal must have flowed abundantly. The Ranger had caught them in a drunken sleep.

Corral gates opened, and horsemen charged out. They couldn't see the Rangers hidden in the brush and the fog. They rode straight into the Ranger guns. The Texans waited for Captain to give the signal. He raised his rifle to his shoulder. In a moment it belched flame, and a rider pitched from his saddle, directly under the hoofs of the other horses. Flame lanced in a ragged pattern from points all up and down the brushline. Horses plunged to the ground, screaming. Men shouted in pain and anger and fright. Some men lay still. A few tried crawling away but were quickly picked off.

Those riders not hit in the first savage volley wheeled their horses around and spurred desperately back toward the stockade. Ranger rifles kept firing, and more *Cortinistas* fell.

In the moments of lull that followed, the Rangers hurriedly strengthened their positions. Lanham moved from his exposed location and threw himself belly-down in a small depression behind a bush. At the stockade, he could see the *Cortinistas* milling in confusion and anger. They came boiling out, charging again without leadership, without purpose. It occurred to Lanham that they still couldn't see the Rangers hidden in the brush. The bandits expected to see mounted men. They rode headlong into the Ranger position.

A second time they met a blistering volley. They were too close to haul around and go back. Those who survived the first shots came spurring, trying to overrun the line. Most of them didn't make it. A few sped past the Rangers, seeing them too late. These, caught behind the line, never had a chance. The Rangers could not afford to let them get away, for they had seen how few the invaders really were.

The lull was longer after the second charge. Down in the corral Lanham saw that more men and more horses were ready. Now he could see the bandits rallying around one man who sat astride a fine horse.

Captain looked through his spyglass. "It's the old man . . . Juan Flores Salinas. They've got a leader now, boys. This time they'll draw blood." From the direction of Camargo, other men were galloping in, drawn to the aid of Las Cuevas by the thunder of the guns.

"Boys," said the captain, "when we lost the surprise, we lost it all. They'll cut us off if we stay here. Let's break for the river. Don't shoot unless you have to."

That was the best suggestion Lanham had heard since supper. He joined the irregular line of running men. Captain stayed back with the five horsemen as a rear guard, giving his Rangers the best of it.

Somehow, though Lanham ran and stumbled and fell and pushed to his feet and ran some more through the sand and brush and angry grabbing of thorns, he didn't tire. His feet didn't hurt anymore. Maybe the direction made the difference. Somewhere ahead of them, hidden by the patchy fog, lay the Rio Grande. With three or four hundred aroused Cuevian bandits behind them, Texas was going to look mighty good . . . if they made it.

He wouldn't have bet much on their getting there. It seemed inevitable that Salinas would send flankers loping around to cut them off, then surround them and begin a systematic annihilation.

But he didn't. Captain's strategy was still working. The bandits had no idea how many invaders had hit them. Surely they must have thought it was several times the actual number, for only lunatics would have attacked a strong position and challenged a force ten times their size. The Mexicans knew by now, of course, that the Rangers were falling back. But they didn't know how far they had gone. The logical supposition was that they had moved only far enough to set up a trap.

The first two charges so terribly lacerated the Cuevians that old Salinas was cautious about riding into a trap and losing more of his force. On horseback, he moved forward no faster than the Rangers were moving backward. No Ranger had fired a shot during the retreat, and no *Cortinista* had as yet actually seen a Ranger in the fog.

The Rangers passed Las Cuchattas, where they had made that mistaken assault. The dead still lay unmoved. At the sight of the Rangers, a few women retreated quickly into their *jacales*. It was as if the whole camp was dead.

Nearing the river, the bandits became bolder, for they realized now they faced a retreating force, not a trap. Captain, in the rear guard, fired a shot and brought down a horseman. Sporadic firing started. The Rangers slowed their retreat, looking back over their shoulders for targets. Reaching the riverbank, they dropped down behind a shallow ledge and faced around, rifles and pistols ready, providing cover for the rear guard. The fog was lifting, burning off under the heat of the morning sun.

The Cuevians spotted the Ranger position. The old *jefe* rallied his men to charge.

Across the river, the U.S. troopers now could see what was going on. The Gatling gun had arrived. A nervous soldier set the gun to firing. The bullets passed over the Rangers' heads, into the ranks of the bandits. Several fell. Salinas signaled a charge, to get down into the lower ground where the Gatling gun couldn't be used for fear of hitting the Rangers.

Lanham watched the heavy line of horsemen thundering toward him through mesquite and willow. His mouth was dry. His heart seemed to be in his throat. His hands were slick with cold sweat as he brought the rifle into line. Across the river, the Gatling gun still chattered. At that distance it did little damage, but it was a comforting sound.

Ranger guns blazed in another volley. The old *jefe* was one of the first to fall, plunging headlong from his silver-studded, big-horned Mexico saddle. The first line of Cuevian horsemen was cut down like a stand of wheat struck by the whispering blade of a scythe. Some of the horses plunged over the bank, around the Rangers. One went straight down into quicksand, screaming as it disappeared. The others cut back. So did the surviving horsemen. They spurred away, the charge broken.

Captain stood up and looked. The fallen chieftain hadn't stirred. The *jefe* of Cortina's western division lay dead in the sand.

"Boys," said Captain, "dig in. I imagine we've stopped them awhile."

Lanham knew then that Captain had no intention of going back across the river. He had come for cattle.

In the long lull, an army officer crossed with two men

in a boat. Other troopers shucked their clothes and swam over to reinforce the McNelly position. Beaching his tiny craft, the officer hurried to McNelly. "When we first heard the shooting, we thought you were all dead."

McNelly smiled grimly. "There are lots of dead, but none of them are ours. We haven't lost a man." He paused, looking wishfully across toward the Gatling gun. "When are the rest of them coming over?"

The officer said soberly, "Except for a few volunteers, I doubt they ever will. Face it, McNelly. The wires are saying you've invaded a sovereign land. The army isn't going to back you."

McNelly frowned. "*You're* backing me."

The officer removed his shoulder straps. "Unofficially, that's all."

The Cuevian force had pulled back out of sight. The Rangers and the underwear-clad soldiers who had come to aid them took advantage of the quiet period to dig holes in the bank and pile up fortifications in front of them. Lanham dug grimly, knowing his life might depend upon it, wondering how long before the bandits nerved themselves for another assault.

The Cuevians didn't make a move. The Rangers finished their digging and settled down to rest. Rest was fine, but it had one disadvantage: it gave them too much time to think. Their situation here was not one Lanham enjoyed thinking about.

After a time, Major Alexander came across in a rowboat. McNelly met him at the bank. "You come to help us?"

Alexander shook his head. "Orders, Captain. I have a telegram here for you from Colonel Potter at Fort Brown. He advises you to retreat at once to the Texas side."

McNelly read the telegram, his eyes narrowing. "He's ordering you to give me no assistance."

"That's right, Captain."

"But I thought . . ."

"So did I. But he's under pressure. Orders are orders, Captain. What answer shall I give him?"

McNelly held silent a moment, chewing his black cigar. Lanham watched intently, for that was a sign the devil was in him. McNelly said, "Tell him no."

"The colonel is already catching hell. He won't be pleased."

"Just the same, tell him no."

Alexander accepted the decision without rancor. "I'll tell him." He started for his boat, then paused. "When did your men last eat?" Told they hadn't eaten since supper, the major said, "I'll send some food over. I don't guess that is the same as military support."

Seeming not to see the soldiers who had scattered among the Rangers, he went back across the river.

During the long afternoon, the Cuevians made sporadic probes at the Ranger lines. Each time, fire from the McNelly men and the soldiers drove them back.

Across the river, the military telegraph was all but smoking. In the early-morning excitement that followed the first sound of gunfire, the young telegraph operator had assumed the worst and reported that McNelly's command was wiped out. Fort Brown had set up a relay system with eastern points and had delivered a report into Washington. Queries and orders began crackling back down the line until they came out at the key beneath the rough telegraph pole where an army signalman had spliced into the border wire. Off and on during the afternoon, an officer would punt the boat across to keep McNelly posted on latest developments. One thing became clear: government officials from Texas to Washington were in a stew about McNelly's position.

So were the Mexicans. From Fort Brown, telegraph communications were sent to the American embassy in

Matamoros, and the messages were relayed to the American official in Mexican Camargo, opposite Rio Grande City, instructing him to oversee McNelly's surrender to proper Mexican authority.

McNelly's reaction was to chew his black cigar ever more vigorously. "Surrender, hell!"

Major Alexander came across in the boat and regretfully gave orders for all remaining troopers to return to the Texas bank. He handed McNelly another telegraph message. "This one," he said, "comes from the top. It's from Belknap himself, the Secretary of War."

McNelly almost bit the cigar in two as he read. "He demands that we retreat at once to Texas. He doesn't ask. He *demands*."

"What answer do you want me to give him?"

McNelly's thin frame was straight and stiff. He dug a piece of brown wrapping paper from his pocket and found a stub pencil. "I'll write him the answer myself. I'll tell him he can take his United States army and go to hell!"

Alone now, the Rangers held their vigil on the quiet bank, listening and watching. At one point a small party came under a flag of truce and picked up the Cuevian dead. There was no sign of assault.

Lieutenant Robinson asked, "Captain, you think they'll try us again?"

Captain nodded. "Probably. They've got to do *something*. They can't just let us stay here."

"How long do you think we can keep standin' them off?"

Captain pondered. "Long enough." He pointed his cigar toward the river. "Those soldiers over yonder, they're on our side, orders or not. They've already come to our aid once. If they see we're about to be wiped out, they'll come again. They'll come in force, despite anything the Secretary of War or anybody else has to say.

That will mean an official unit of the United States army has invaded Mexican soil. And that, Lieutenant, is an act of war."

The lieutenant's jaw dropped. "Captain, are you tryin' to start a war with Mexico?"

Captain smiled grimly. "The Mexican government has gone to sleep and let Cortina take complete control on the border because they've got bigger things on their mind to worry about. They know he's bloodthirsty; they know he's corrupt. Still, he's just a little problem compared to all the others they've got. But give them the threat of war with the United States and all of a sudden Cortina is a problem—the biggest one they have. They'll have to move quick. If we can get the United States army over here, we can force the Mexican government itself to stop Cortina."

The lieutenant stared in awe. "Captain, this is too audacious even for *you*. With thirty men, you're tryin' to force the hands of two governments."

"Thirty *good* men," McNelly pointed out. "And well-placed."

"Cortina may be corrupt, but he's also intelligent. Think he won't realize the spot you've placed him in?"

McNelly shrugged. "If he does, so much the better. He'll have more respect for us from now on. A lot more respect. He'll know that what we've done once, we can do again."

Lanham Neal silently shook his head and looked down at his shaking hand. If he lived to be a hundred and six, he would always believe Captain had had this whole thing planned before he ever crossed the river.

Twenty-one

CAPTAIN MCNELLY HAD TAKEN THE boat to the Texas side to send messages on the military wire when the flag of truce showed up. Five horsemen rode out into the open. Four were Mexicans, one a *gringo.*

Lieutenant Robinson had been left in charge. He watched distrustfully until the riders brought their white flag out well into a clearing that lay between the riverbank and the heavy brush beyond. "Sergeant Hall, you hustle over and notify Captain. I'll take four men, and we'll parley till Captain gets here."

He picked four nearby Rangers. Lanham Neal was one. They moved out, rifles carried at the ready. Walking, Lanham warily eyed the *gringo.* "Lieutenant, do you know him?"

Robinson nodded. "Doc Headly. He's on Captain's 'wanted' list if ever he steps over to the Texas side. He's a *Cortinista.*"

The horsemen stopped and waited. Lanham could see that the *gringo* carried a carbine. A piece of paper was clamped in its hammer. The *gringo*'s eyes were suspicious. "I've got a message here for the commanding officer."

"I am the commanding officer," said the lieutenant.

"You're not McNelly. I want to see McNelly."

"McNelly's across the river. I'm in command till he gets back."

Headly nodded. "Then I reckon while we wait for him, we'd just as well stand easy." He reached into a nosebag tied to his saddle and fetched out a bottle of mescal. "How about a little smile?"

Robinson said, "I never drink while I'm on duty."

"A pity." The renegade doctor offered the bottle to the other Rangers, who turned him down, then tilted it for a long, long swallow. He passed it on to the Mexicans who flanked him. "Man never knows when the next drink is coming. He ought never to turn one down."

By the time McNelly came, the bottle was almost drained and a flush had risen in the *gringo*'s face. "McNelly," he said arrogantly, "do you know who I am?"

"I do," the captain replied evenly. "Your name is known to every peace officer from Austin to the river."

Headly's eyes showed a beginning of anger. "Do you realize what you've done? You've unlawfully invaded a peace-loving sovereign nation, and you've killed honest, peaceful citizens. One of them was the *alcalde* himself, the beloved Juan Flores Salinas. Have you any idea how many good citizens of Mexico you've killed today?"

McNelly said he didn't. The *gringo* said, "Close to eighty."

McNelly frowned. "Is that all? I hoped it was more."

"This is a grave situation. Your action is unexcusable. It has put relations in a very precarious position between the United States and the Republic of Mexico."

"I didn't come all the way out here to listen to a harangue. You've got a letter under that hammer. If it's for me, let me have it. If it's not, I suggest you get the hell away from here."

Headly extended the carbine to McNelly, butt first, so the captain could take the letter. "It is from the chief justice himself, representing the state of Tamaulipas."

Lanham watched the captain's face, and he could guess what the letter said. He figured that a man who would tell the United States Secretary of War to go to hell would have even choicer words for the chief justice of a robber pueblo.

"What's your answer?" Headly demanded.

"I came to get those Texas cattle. I'll stay till we have them."

"I may as well tell you. Three full regiments of Mexican troops are on their way here from Monterrey and from Matamoros to drive you out of Mexico."

"You'll need them all," said McNelly.

Headly's eyes narrowed. "You're foolish, Captain. How many men do you have with you?"

Listening, Lanham realized the bandits still had no idea how many Rangers lay waiting beyond that bank. They were fishing for information.

"Enough," the captain said, "to march to Mexico City!"

Lanham heard a voice and turned. A Ranger came running, rifle in hand. "Captain! Captain, there's men yonder a-horseback, fannin' out around you. They don't aim to let you get back to the bank."

Lanham's breath stopped momentarily. He could sense rather than see the movement, obscured by the brush.

Tightly the captain barked, "All right, boys, each of you draw a bead. If any one of those bandits fires a shot, all five men on this truce team are to die. And Headly is mine!"

Looking down the muzzle of McNelly's pistol, the *gringo* swallowed. His flushed face went almost purple. To one of the Mexicans he said in Spanish, "Tell them to back away. Tell them under no circumstances is any man to shoot."

The Mexican seemed extremely happy to go and deliver the message, away from point-blank range of the Texan guns. The Cuevians pulled off.

"Now," said the captain, letting the pistol sag a little— but not too far—"you came out here to treat with me. You're going to treat. I want those cattle back. Every single head. Not one of us is leaving here till we've come to an agreement. Not you, and not me."

Headly blustered and fumed. Captain reminded him the Rangers had come prepared for war and would press it as far as was necessary. Moreover, the United States army waited just across the river. The bandits already had had a taste of their Gatling gun. Would they like a sample closer at hand? Would they like a full-scale war with all the power of the United States to press it?

In the end Headly took a long swig from what little was left of the mescal. "The cattle are penned at Camargo."

"I don't care where they're penned. I want them in Texas. If you want to leave here without a war, you'll write out an order now and sign it. Otherwise, we'll attack within the hour!"

Headly's hands shook so much he couldn't write. McNelly wrote the order for him, on his own terms. "This specifies," he pointed out, "that the cattle are to be delivered to the Texas side of the river tomorrow morning opposite Camargo. No excuses, no exceptions. All the cattle!"

The *gringo* signed the order in a wobbly hand. He

finished the bottle and turned away like a whipped dog.

Captain said, "Tomorrow morning. If the cattle aren't there, we'll be back."

The truce party rode away.

McNelly walked to the riverbank, elated. "Boys, we've done it. We've met them on their own ground and whipped them down. Let's go back to our own side of the river."

Relief and jubilation was the mood of the Rangers as they set their boots victoriously back on the Texas side to the cheers of waiting soldiers and a considerable gathering of *gringo* and Mexican civilians, drawn by word of the fighting. They ate a hearty supper of beef, brought by a nearby *ranchero* who still had a few cattle left the bandits hadn't stolen. Then they saddled and rode to a point opposite Camargo, near Rio Grande City.

The longer Lanham Neal thought about the situation, the less sure he was. They were on the north bank again and the Cuevians still had the cattle on the south bank. An agreement with bandits was worth only whatever the bandits considered it to be worth. Lanham lay on his blanket, looking across at the flickering candlelight that marked Camargo. He didn't sleep much.

He had lost track of time, but somebody told him next morning that it was Sunday. He could see the cattle pens, well beyond the bank across the river. A mile, maybe, but it could as well have been a hundred, if the Cuevians didn't choose to deliver. The armed riders around the pole corrals were not a hopeful sign.

After breakfast, Captain McNelly walked down to the ferry landing with a note to Diego Garcia, who would be in command now that Salinas was dead. It asked for early delivery of the cattle as specified in the agreement signed by Headly. Presently a Mexican messenger was back with a reply. It seemed, he said, everyone had over-

looked the fact that this was Sunday. No business could
be conducted on the Sabbath.

Captain began chewing the cigar. "The business was
conducted yesterday," he said. "Now I want those
cattle."

Negotiations were carried back and forth through the
morning by way of emissaries with no sign of success.
After treating his Rangers to a dinner of coffee and *pan
dulces*, Captain took them all back down to the river and
counted off ten men closest to hand. It was Lanham's
dubious fortune to be standing there in front.

"We're going over," he said, "and wind up the negotiations."

The ferry ride was slow. Lanham looked into the
muddy water, bleakly wondering why the hell he had
ever given in to the moment of weakness that had made
a Ranger of him. The first trip across that river had been
risk enough. A second trip looked like suicide.

His feelings were shared. He heard one of the Rangers
murmur, "I'd as soon not be a part of this Death
Squad."

The captain was calmly talking to the old ferryman,
asking him if he had been to church.

I wish I'd gone to church this morning, Lanham thought.
In San Antonio or someplace.

*The least Captain could have done was to bring the whole
company*, he worried. *Thirty men can put up a lot more fight
than ten.*

But as the ferry neared the Mexico bank, he began to
see the captain's reason. Sight of all those Rangers would
have alarmed the Cuevians and brought reinforcements
on the run. The ten created no stir. Only a handful of
customs officials and Rurales waited at the ferry landing.

Captain stepped off first and hitched the ferry's rope
to a post. He walked serenely toward the waiting officers.
They wore uniforms of the Mexican government, but
they were Cortina's men. Their allegiance was to him,

not to Mexico City. Captain picked out the one who appeared to be in charge. "I have come for the cattle."

The officer seemed annoyed. "Has it not been made plain to you? This is Sunday. It is not proper to do work on the Sabbath."

The gate of the corral was open, and the cattle were being driven out. They were being pointed south, not north toward the river. Before this Sabbath was over, they would be far away.

Captain said: "I have a paper duly signed by an officer, and I took it he was a gentleman. He agreed the cattle would be delivered today. No word was said about the Sabbath."

"I am in charge here, not he," the official said stiffly. "It is impossible to deliver the cattle today. Even if it were not the Sabbath, no duty has been paid on these cattle. Duty must be paid before they can cross into Texas."

"No duty was paid when they crossed into Mexico *from* Texas," McNelly pointed out, "and by the Eternal none will be paid now."

The captain moved with the quickness of a panther. He threw the customs officer to the ground and shoved his knee into the man's belly, jamming the muzzle of a pistol against his head. The Rangers, startled, swung their weapons to cover the Rurales and the other customs men.

"Now, you mealy-mouthed son of a bitch," the captain gritted, "you'll honor that agreement or die!"

The officer sputtered in surprise and panic. "Take the cattle! Take the cattle!"

"No, we're not going to take them. The agreement was that they would be delivered. You're going to lie here with my pistol against your head till they're across that river. One bad move from anybody and I'll scatter your brains in the sand. What's more, we'll kill every scoundrel here."

One officer was allowed to ride out to the herd and give the order. The Rangers held their ground, watching as the Cuevian *vaqueros* stripped off their clothes, herded the cattle into the Rio Grande and swam them across. Not until they saw the herd shaking of the muddy water on the Texas bank did McNelly release his hold on the customs officer and motion for his men to return to the ferry.

In the slow calm of the crossing, Lanham Neal found himself trembling, a reaction to the tension that had ended. He gazed at the serene little captain, who stood on the forward end of the ferry. Captain was dog-tired, face colorless, but his teeth were clamped jubilantly on a cigar that was pointed straight up in victory.

Cortina doesn't rule the border anymore, Lanham thought. *McNelly does. When Cortina is gone and forgotten, they'll still remember McNelly.*

On the Texas bank, a throng of people waited—Rangers, soldiers, civilians, cheering wildly. In all the years of the border raiding, this was the first herd of stolen cattle that had ever come out of Mexico back into Texas. This was a whipping from which the border bandits would never recover.

Far away in his Matamoros stronghold, Cortina probably didn't realize it yet, but this was the day that had broken his back.

Just before the ferry touched the bank, McNelly turned to his men. "Meet them proudly, boys. We went over there with our heads and our backs up. We've returned the same way."

Twenty-two

ON THE RIVERBANK, LANHAM NEAL found Vincente de Zavala and Bonifacio Holguín waiting for him. Bonifacio rushed forward and gave him the *abrazo*. "*Caporál*, I heard you were killed."

Lanham tried to smile, but it wasn't in him. "I'm still here."

"They said at the *rancho* . . ." Bonifacio broke off and turned his face away to avoid the shame of tears.

Vincente looked grave. "Bonifacio has brought news, *caporál*. About *la patrona*. It is not good."

"What about Zoe? Somethin' happened to her?"

Bonifacio faced around slowly, his gaze on Lanham's boots. "It is the new *patrón*, the Bailey, her husband. He is crazy with jealousy, *caporál*. A traveler brought news from Las Cuevas crossing that all the Rangers had been killed. *La patrona*, she cried much, for she knew you were with them. The Bailey, he was much angry over her crying. He beat her. Now, *caporál*, it is good for a man to beat his wife a little bit once in a while, for this keeps her happy with him and shows he loves her. But the Bailey, he beat *la patrona* much more than a little. She fought him, and he beat her until she was almost dead.

"It is whispered among the *vaqueros* that it was Bailey himself who killed his first wife. It is whispered that he will kill *la patrona* also, if he beats her again. He has her land. He knows now that he cannot ever have her love. Her love is for you. It always has been."

"She married *him*," Lanham said.

"At a time of foolish pride. She is her father's daughter, and the Daingerfield, he was always a stubborn man. She is much woman. Once you had much love for her. I think you have it yet, from your face."

"Bailey's her husband. I got no right."

Vincente de Zavala put in a contribution. "If he killed her, *caporál*, you would then kill him, *no es verdad?*"

Lanham nodded soberly. "I reckon I would."

"Then stop him now, *before* he kills her. You will save yourself much trouble."

When it was put that way, Lanham could see enough logic in it to justify himself. He had known from the first that he wasn't going to stand by and do nothing. He went to McNelly.

"Captain, I got to ask you for leave. There's somethin' I got to do. Somethin' personal."

McNelly was not that lax. He had to have particulars, and Lanham was obliged to give him the whole story. McNelly rubbed his beard, troubled. "Neal, I can respect your concern, but this is something between a man and his wife. It's not something in which the Rangers have any right to intrude."

"I wouldn't be goin' as a Ranger, sir. I'd be goin' as Lanham Neal."

"You'd have to resign. I couldn't allow the Rangers

to become entangled in a family problem, much as I might want to."

Lanham said regretfully, "Then, sir, I reckon I better turn in my resignation. I'll be leavin' directly." He paused. "Sir, before I go, there's one thing I just got to say."

"What's that, Neal?"

"Captain, you're no carpetbagger!"

Riding up to the ranch headquarters, flanked by Vincente and Bonifacio, Lanham Neal watched the Bailey barns and main house carefully. He had no particular plan. He meant to go directly to the house and see about Zoe. Whatever Bailey decided to do, Lanham would meet that problem as it arose.

The dark Rafael and another *vaquero* were shoeing a horse in a corral. Lanham was close enough to recognize the animal. One of Griffin Daingerfield's. It hadn't taken Bailey long to exercise his property rights. The *vaqueros* straightened and watched as Lanham and his *compadres* rode to the house. One of them dropped a hammer and trotted into the barn.

Lanham swung down from the saddle. "Remember, boys, anything that happens between me and Bailey is our fight, not yours. All I want you to do is keep his *vaqueros* off of me."

"He may kill you, *caporál*," Vincente said.

"If he does, then do what you want to." Lanham paused on the front gallery and lifted his pistol halfway out of the holster, then let it slip back. He wanted to be sure it would draw easy if he needed it. "Zoe!" he called. "It's me, Lanham. I'm comin' in!"

He stepped through the door, blinking in the dim light. He heard a woman's startled cry before he saw her. Zoe stood in a bedroom doorway, a pistol in her hand. She let it sag.

"Lanham? Lanham?" She cried out as she stumbled toward him. He saw the ugly bruises and the swollen eye before she fell into his arms. "They told me you were dead," she sobbed.

"I'm here, Zoe. I come to help you."

"Lanham, I tried my best to hate you, but I couldn't. I still loved you, even when I was bein' a fool."

"I come to take you away from here, if you want to go."

"Yes, I want to go. I want to go home. Take me before I kill him, or he kills me."

"Home's not far enough. He'll come after you."

"He'll wish he hadn't. I've made up my mind that he won't ever touch me again. Me, or anything that belongs to me."

"We could go to the Panhandle or someplace, far off, where he couldn't reach you."

Zoe was still a Daingerfield. "That land is mine," she said stubbornly. "I'd rather die than leave it for him. Take me home, Lanham."

She hadn't changed, and suddenly he realized he never wanted her to. He drew her fiercely into his arms, still wanting her as desperately as ever. "Throw some things together, Zoe. We'll get out of here."

He heard heavy boots strike the wooden gallery, and he knew Bailey must have been at the barn. "Neal!" Bailey roared. "Neal, I know you're in there. You come out here, right now."

Lanham pushed Zoe aside. All the way over here, he had vacillated between a hope that Bailey would be gone and they would miss him, and one that he would be here with his back up so Lanham could give him everything he had coming to him. The first wish had won out in the final test of judgment.

Lanham looked out the front window. He couldn't see Bailey, but he could see that Vincente and Bonifacio were holding Rafael and half a dozen *vaqueros* off to a neutral distance. The fight would be between Lanham and Bailey . . . them alone.

Lanham had a strong conviction that if he stepped to that door, Bailey would blow a hole in him. Looking around for another way out, he saw a second door in the far end of the parlor. It opened onto the gallery but just around the corner.

"Bailey," Lanham called, "I come to take Zoe away from here."

"She belongs to me. You can't touch her. She's mine like the land is mine, and the cattle, and the horses. Touch her and I got a husband's right to kill you. The law can't lift a finger."

"You beat her, Bailey. Law don't give you a right to do that."

"What I done is between me and her. The Rangers fixin' to step in between a man and his wife?"

"I'm not here as a Ranger. I quit. I'm here as a friend to get her out of your reach."

"Or just to get her, maybe? She's damaged goods, Neal. Somebody else besides you has had her now. Even if you was to have her again, you couldn't forget that."

Zoe stood in the bedroom doorway, face stricken in fear. "Maybe he's right, Lanham. Maybe you couldn't forget that."

"And then again," said Lanham, "maybe I could." He weighed the distance to the door at the other end of the room. He picked up a lamp from a table and hefted it, getting the feel of its weight and balance. "Bailey," he shouted, "I'm comin' out. Let's talk it over."

"Come on," said Bailey.

Lanham hurled the lamp at the facing of the front door and turned on his heel, sprinting for the other door. He was halfway there when the lamp shattered. He heard the boom of Bailey's pistol, like a cannon the way it echoed in the room. He had been right; Bailey was poised to shoot him the moment he stepped into view.

But Lanham was out the side door as Bailey fired a second shot in reflex. Lanham had his own pistol in his hand. He hove around the corner. Bailey saw him from the tail of his eye and swung, pistol coming up for another shot.

Lanham didn't hesitate. McNelly had taught him better. He squeezed the trigger once and then again. Bailey slammed back against the gallery railing, eyes big in surprise. Steadying himself, he began bringing the pistol up again. He moved slowly, agonizingly.

Those two were for Zoe, Lanham thought coldly. *This one is for your other wife.* He fired once more, and Bailey went over the railing.

Bailey's *vaqueros* made no hostile move. They were still under the guns of Vincente and Bonifacio.

Lanham walked across the gallery to look down at Bailey. He became aware of a crackling noise and jerked around. One of Bailey's shots must have struck sparks off of something. The kerosene from the shattered lamp was going into flame. Lanham rushed into the house and looked around urgently for something to beat out the fire.

Zoe stopped him. "It's a miserable house. All it's ever known was pain and fear. Let it burn."

Lanham shrugged. "I reckon it's yours to do with as you want to. He's dead."

Zoe had time to gather a few belongings before the flames reached the point of danger. She carried them onto the gallery on the side away from the fire. Outside, in the daylight, Lanham saw more plainly how she had been beaten. He hadn't had time yet to regret killing Bailey. Now he was sure he never would.

The Bailey *vaqueros* were getting nervous, wanting to

do something about the fire. Lanham raised his hand. "She is *la patrona*. She says let it burn."

Rafael and another *vaquero* grabbed Bailey by the legs and dragged him clear of the flames. By the casual way they did it, Lanham knew they had been attached to him only by wages, not by any regard. Lanham had nothing to fear from them now.

"Vincente, Bonifacio, you can put your guns up. Let's get away from this heat."

In minutes the house was swallowed in flames. Zoe buried her face against Lanham's chest. "I don't want to look. I don't ever want to see it again. I just want to get away from here."

"You're his widow. The place belongs to you now."

"Not by rights. In a way, he stole it from Josefa's family, marryin' her just to get it. They can have it back. I never want to set foot on it again."

"You're givin' away a lot."

"I still got a place of my own." She looked up at him and corrected herself. "We have a place of *our* own, Lanham. Whatever belongs to me belongs to you." When Lanham didn't say anything, she went on anxiously, "Maybe you don't want that place anymore. You said we might go to the Panhandle. All right, we could do that. We could sell the ranch and go fresh. We could leave this border country and never look back, if that's what you want to do. Only, take me with you, Lanham. Don't leave me here by myself."

He still didn't answer. She cried out, "Lanham, say something. Say you want me, or say you don't want me. Say *something* so I'll know you've heard me."

He nodded soberly and held her tighter. "I heard you, Zoe; I was just thinkin'. I was thinkin' that a lot of blood has been spilled on this Nueces Strip for us to run away and leave it now. Your daddy's . . . lots of people's. And Captain . . . he's just about broke what health he had left. He's got death in his face now; I doubt he'll live out the winter. If we was to leave now, it'd be like sayin' that was all for nothin', like it didn't mean nothin' to us. But it *does* mean somethin', Zoe. It means I'm stayin'. *You're* stayin'. There's been too high a price paid for us to leave."

"We don't have a lot to start on, Lanham. A piece of land, a couple of mud shacks and what few cattle the bandits didn't steal."

"There's somethin' else ... my Ranger wages I've saved up. I got over a hundred dollars I didn't spend."

"A hundred dollars!" He could feel her tears soaking through his shirt and touching warm against his skin. "With all that to start on, nobody can stop us. We're rich!"

Kelton on Kelton

I WAS BORN AT A PLACE CALLED HORSE Camp on the Scharbauer Cattle Company's Five Wells Ranch in Andrews County, Texas, in 1926. My father was a cowboy there, and my grandfather was the ranch foreman. My great-grandfather had come out from East Texas about 1876 with a wagon and a string of horses to become a ranchman, but he died young, leaving four small boys to grow up as cowpunchers and bronc breakers. With all that heritage I should have become a good cowboy myself, but somehow I never did, so I decided if I could not do it I would write about it.

I studied journalism at the University of Texas and became a livestock and farm reporter in San Angelo, Texas, writing fiction as a sideline to newspaper work. I have maintained the two careers in parallel for forty-two years. My fiction has been mostly about Texas, about areas whose history and people I know from long study and long personal acquaintance. I have always believed we can learn much about ourselves by studying our history, for we are the products of all that has gone before us. All history is relevant today, because the way we live—the values we believe in—are a result of molds prepared for us by our forebears a long time ago.

I was an infantryman in World War II and married an Austrian girl, Anna, I met there shortly after the war. We raised three children, all grown now and independent, proud of their mixed heritage of the Old World on one hand and the Texas frontier on the other.